ORPHAN TRAIN CHRISTMAS

RACHEL WESSON

CHAPTER 1

DECEMBER 5TH, 1895

"We can't give every child a perfect Christmas. We have to focus on those we can help."

Lily set aside the scarf she was attempting to knit. She glanced at the pile of presents Kathleen was sorting into small piles on the side table. "I'm worried about you, Kathleen. You haven't been yourself since Thanksgiving. I know it wasn't the day you'd hoped for, but we did our best, given the circumstances."

Kathleen knew Lily was right. They had a lot to be thankful for. The children destined to go on the orphan train had escaped New York before the worst of the outbreak of cholera. It hadn't been as bad as the epidemic of 1892, but it was serious enough to result in many deaths.

"Kathleen, last Thursday was never going to be as special as previous Thanksgivings. The staff were missing the children who left, and we had the little ones to deal with. George, who lost both his parents and—"

Kathleen interrupted quickly. "I know I am being selfish and silly, but I just wanted it to be a good day. We have so much to be thankful for. Bridget surviving her illness, Bella's and Brian's wedding, the placements for the children. I feel guilty for being upset, but we had such a lovely day planned. Richard missed it due to his work at the hospital. You had to stay away for fear of falling sick, and… Oh, listen to me. I am being so whiny, aren't I?"

Lily smiled her gentle smile, but her eyes were filled with concern.

"Kathleen, I think you are overtired, and it is normal to be emotional. You were a real trooper over the last few weeks. If it weren't for Sheila and Cook and you nursing all those who fell ill, the death toll would have been much higher. We didn't lose one child. Who else can say that? You beat the Cholera, and those children owe you and the rest of our ladies their lives."

"Father Nelson and the boys, Tommy and Mike, played their parts, too. If only the city officials would listen to Father Nelson and others like him. If the tenements were cleaned up and weren't so overcrowded, the disease wouldn't spread so fast. We aren't asking for much, just clean water and good food for everyone."

Kathleen knew she was repeating everything Lily believed in and fought so hard for. Some days the fight just seemed too hard, and today was one of them.

"You can't give up now. I won't let you. Yes, the others did their bit, but you showed true leadership throughout the whole ordeal. You lead by example and showed maturity beyond your years. I am very proud of you, and I know Bridget is, too." Lily fell silent for a few seconds, possibly to gather her thoughts and to keep from falling into the same melancholy Kathleen was feeling. "We have to learn to celebrate small victories. Big change comes after a series of small changes. So, for now, we have to forget the bigger problems. We just have to work on making Christmas special. The children are missing their friends who left on the train, and those who lost family members are obviously upset. We must do our best to give them a good Christmas."

CHAPTER 2

*K*athleen knew Lily was right and resolved to do her best to get into the Christmas spirit.

"When will Bridget arrive?" Lily asked, obviously trying to lighten the mood.

"Carl sent a telegram to say they hoped to be here tomorrow. They stopped over to see Jacob and Lizzie and also to catch up with Sally. I can't wait to see them."

"Me, too," Lily agreed. "But I hope it won't be too difficult for Bridget to see me like this. And the twins."

Kathleen wasn't sure how Bridget

would cope, but knowing her sister, she would be happy for Lily. "You know Bridget. She wouldn't let anything dim her joy for Charlie and you. It's not your fault she can't have children."

"I know, but it's hard to accept that. She is such a natural mother. I wish things had worked out differently for her."

"So do I, but at least she is alive. We have to count our blessings," Kathleen responded, but did she really believe what she was saying? It was difficult to accept God's will sometimes. Some people had children so easily, even those that didn't want them. Others, like Bridget and Carl, who desperately wanted to be parents, couldn't.

They heard sounds of children fighting upstairs in the bedrooms. Kathleen stood up.

"You stay where you are and rest. I will see what's going on. Are you hungry? Can I fetch you a sandwich?"

Lily laughed. "I know you all think I am a glutton, but I can't help it. I am starving all the time now. A sandwich sounds good. Can you ask Cook to put in some of her pickles and some apple slices with the ham?"

Kathleen rolled her eyes. Lily's unusual sandwich combinations made everyone smile, but Cook insisted on making them just the way Lily asked. Regardless of how stomach churning they seemed to everyone else.

CHAPTER 3

The children had finally settled down for the evening, and Lily had enjoyed her pickle, apple, and ham sandwich. Kathleen had settled for a plain ham and was sitting at the fire, toasting her feet. Charlie would arrive soon to take Lily home. She glanced at the pile of presents on the table.

"Do you think we will have enough for all of them?" Kathleen asked, her teeth nibbling her lower lip.

"Kathleen, the children will be thrilled. Most of them haven't seen an orange before, let alone had a whole one to themselves. Cook is baking sweets—she let me taste her chocolate fudge, and it is amazing. Those are the presents the kids will like most. They may benefit from the socks and gloves and warm underclothes, but they won't be jumping up and down with excitement, because they got an extra pair of socks."

Kathleen knew Lily was right, but she wanted this Christmas to be perfect. Only George, one of the orphans who had lost his parents to the cholera outbreak and was currently living at the sanctuary, had seen a Christmas tree before and remembered getting gifts from Santa. The other children didn't have such nice memories. They would be leaving New York in January on the next orphan train, and she wanted them to leave with good memories.

"Have you finished the paperwork for Father Nelson, Kathleen?"

"I have the cards for the new orphans to do yet, but the rest is done. I have made a list of all the placements we made in the last year. Thankfully, Bridget and Carl adopted their own recommendations and kept such records. It's a pity it took the committee so long to agree to their suggestions."

"Yes, it is, but committees take a long time to agree on anything. Charlie went to a few of the meetings, and he said they seemed most worried about the extra costs involved in checking on the children placed with families."

Kathleen sighed. Her sister and brother-in-law had come up with several recommendations to protect the orphans leaving New York and other places. Having seen for themselves how hit and miss the placements could be, they had suggested to Father Nelson and his co-committee members different ways to protect the children. But it always came down to a question of money. Some people believed money was more important than a child.

"Can't they see we would have fewer orphans running away if the families were vetted before the children were placed? I know it isn't realistic to check on every family who takes a child, but I believe Carl was right when he said the mere threat of being checked on would be enough to ensure some families treat the children better."

"We have to accept small victories," Lily told her. "The committee agreed to the families being vetted by the senior members of the town, be it the priest, pastor, or mayor. Each child will have a record of their placement now, so they can be traced in the future should family members appear. It is better than it used to be."

"But it isn't perfect. There are still families taking children who shouldn't own a skunk."

Lily smiled at the reference before moving forward, a serious expression on her face. "Nothing is ever perfect, Kathleen. We have to work with what we have and be grateful for forward-thinking people like Carl and others for pushing good ideas through. You should stop being so hard on yourself."

"I don't want any of our children being subjected to the abuse my brothers endured. Look at Michael. He's spending Christmas in jail. He wouldn't have ended up there if a good family had taken him in."

"I love you like a sister, but you know that's not true. Michael was in trouble before he ever left New York."

athleen knew Lily was right, but she didn't want to admit it. She didn't want to think about Michael, because then she thought about Shane, and he was even more of a disappointment. She started counting the gifts again, mentally matching them with each child. This Christmas would be fabulous.

"Have you asked Richard if he wants to have Christmas dinner with us and the children? Charlie and Carl will enjoy his company. Father Nelson may join us this year as well, depending on what he has going on in the church."

Kathleen could feel the heat rising from her neck into her cheeks at the mention of the doctor, even though Lily was the only other person in the room.

She hadn't told Lily Richard had declared his feelings on the train when they brought Shane back to New York. Since then, Richard had never mentioned the subject again. He seemed set on staying in New York, and she still wanted to go live in Riverside Springs with her sisters and Bella. Didn't she?

"You haven't asked him yet, have you? What are you waiting for?" Lily exclaimed. "I know you haven't seen much of him over the last few weeks. He's been working himself into an early grave. He and you are cut from the same cloth."

Kathleen knew Richard had worked harder than anyone during the outbreak, with no regard for his own personal safety.

He had taught her a lot about caring for patients suffering from cholera, and she had no doubt he was the reason the children had all survived. He really was a hero, and she loved him. But she couldn't just tell him her feelings had changed. Could she? Surely, she should wait for him to say something first. What if he had changed his mind?

"Lily, I can't. The man is supposed to do the courting, and I feel as if I am chasing him."

Lily burst out laughing, causing Kathleen to stare at her.

"Kathleen, you can be so dim at times. Why do you think he spends so much time here at the sanctuary? I mean, before everyone fell sick. The man was here so often, I was tempted to ask him to move in."

Lily smiled at her own joke. There was a clear no-men-allowed rule at the home, and Lily took the reputation of her sanctuary very seriously.

"He comes to check on the children to make sure they are healthy," Kathleen said. "You know that."

"Before the outbreak, those kids were the healthiest orphans we ever had. Richard has no reason to come visiting, apart from the fact that a certain young lady lives here. He couldn't make it plainer."

Kathleen squirmed in her seat. She wanted Lily to be right, as her feelings for Richard had grown in the sixteen months she had known him. At first, she was grateful for his kindness to Patrick, the orphan she had met on her trip west, and then to her brothers. That was why she had hesitated when he first declared his interest. She thought it was just gratitude on her part. She knew now her feelings had deepened. It wasn't just a physical attraction, although she thought him very handsome. He was also kind and funny and caring and wonderful in so many ways. She had seen how hard he worked and how much he cared for those around him, particularly the little ones.

Lily wasn't letting her off the hook. "Didn't he ask you to numerous shows and events over the summer?" Lily asked.

"Yes, he asks me to speak about the orphans, how difficult the trip on the trains can be, and how damaging it is to be overlooked in town after town. He says I help him to raise funds for the cause."

Lily blew her hair out of her face, as she often did when she was exasperated over something. "You spend a lot of time together. Have you let him know how you feel? Not by telling him, but with gestures. Maybe he is shy."

Richard, shy? Kathleen didn't think so, but was he waiting for her to bring up their past conversation? He'd said he'd wait however long it took, but maybe she had taken too much time to realize her feelings. Had she lost him?

He did spend a lot of time with her. He was passionate about children receiving the best care possible and often told her about his arguments with senior doctors at the hospital. He spent hours trying to convince his peers to spend a couple of hours a week seeing patients who couldn't afford their fees. He often complained his fellow doctors couldn't see a person's worth unless it was attached to a wallet full of cash.

Sometimes, she thought he might say something about their conversation on the train. She had caught him staring at her a few times, and he often held her hand, even when he didn't need to. The other night, when he helped her out of the cab, he had held her waist for a few seconds longer than necessary.

She wished Bridget were here. She could talk to her sister and ask her. Lily was a very good friend, but she was biased. She knew Richard and liked him. In Lily's head, she had them already married off.

"Lily, stop matchmaking. Now, I said I would help with the Christmas tree decorations. Do you want to come up to the sewing room?"

"You can run from me but not from your heart, Kathleen Collins," Lily teased, before putting her hand on her bump. "I think I best stay here. Junior is kicking me again. I swear he will walk out of there himself, if he gets any bigger."

Kathleen could see how tired her friend was. Maybe Lily would nap if she were alone.

"Put the knitting down and close your eyes for a few minutes. The children would love to see you later, if you feel up to it. They want you to pick out the best decoration from the ones they made for the tree."

Lily smiled, but her eyes were already closing. Kathleen pulled a blanket over her friend and left her to rest. She wondered what was keeping Charlie, as he was later than usual. Knowing him, he had gotten caught up studying. He had decided to take his law exams and was working hard, when time became available. As she walked toward the sewing room, Kathleen wondered if Lily was right. Was Richard waiting for a sign from her? How could she tell him she was in love with him? It wasn't something you just announced. Not if you were a well-brought-up lady, someone a doctor would want for his wife.

CHAPTER 5

Mary Clark threw a glance over her shoulder to make sure nobody was following her as she moved deeper into the dark alley.

"Kenny? Are you there?" she whispered, trying to find her brother without bringing the attention of any of the gang members to her. She didn't want to be caught alone in a dark alley by any of them. She had heard the whispers of what they would do to a lone victim.

Where was her brother? He knew better than to be out this late at night. It was dark, and the temperature had dropped. Mary pulled her shawl tighter around her shoulders, although it offered little protection. She thought longingly of her coat, even though it had been too small for her. But her ma had sold it two weeks ago. If the money had been used for food, Mary wouldn't have minded as much.

She dismissed the thoughts from her mind. It was pointless worrying about a lost coat, especially as her five-year-old brother was missing on a freezing night.

"Kenny come on out. This isn't a game. We got to get home, or Ma will be furious. I'm freezin'. I promise ya, Kenny. I will leather your backside myself if you don't tell me where you are."

She heard a sound up ahead. Her heart slowed as she struggled not to turn and race away, back to the relative safety of the area around the tenement where they lived.

"Mary," a pitifully low voice called out.

She rushed forward, all fear for herself forgotten. She slipped in a pile of dirty slush, grazing her knee, but she ignored the sharp pain. Pushing aside a trash can, she found her brother, lying unmoving on the ground, a soft blanket of snow covering his lower body. Was he dead? Terror made her voice harsh.

"Kenny? What happened to you? You've been fighting again, haven't ya? Ma is going to kill ya." Mary pulled her younger brother to his feet as she spoke.

"It wasn't me fault, Mary. They was kickin' Jack, and he's too little to defend hisself. They were mean, real mean, but I got them back. I kicked them hard."

Mary ruffled her brother's hair, as she ran her eyes over his body. His coat, not much better than a ball of rags, was hanging off his shoulder by a thread. His scraped knees showed through his pants, and he'd lost a shoe. But it was the gash on his forehead she was most worried about. He brushed away the blood with his sleeve almost subconsciously.

She tore a piece from her underskirt. It

wasn't exactly clean, but it was the best she could do. She had to tidy him up before they went home, or Ma would have a fit. She pressed the cloth hard against his wound, despite his protests.

"I got to stop the bleeding, so quit squirming." He winced, as she nursed him. In an effort to distract him from the pain, she asked, "So where is this Jack? Does he live around here?"

"Sort of," Kenny answered, his eyes darting to a newspaper on the ground. She followed his gaze, jumping when the paper moved. Before she could stop him, Kenny swooped down and gathered something in his arms.

"This is Jack." Kenny thrust his shoulders out as he held out a pitiful excuse of a dog. Her brother was watching her closely, so she did her best to hide her horrified reaction. The puppy was skin and bones and had nearly as many lacerations on his body as Kenny did. She was about to tell Kenny to put it back where he had found it when the puppy opened his eyes. Big, chocolate-brown eyes captured her heart, just as surely as Kenny had done when he was born five years previously.

"Ah, the poor little mite. He looks like he hasn't been fed in a month of Sundays," she said, putting her hand out to the puppy. She knew better than to try to pat the dog. He had to get used to her first. He sniffed and then moved closer to her. She didn't for a second think the attraction was anything but the smell of the bread roll she had eaten for lunch. He licked her hand, tickling her.

"Kenny, you can't keep him, you know. You have to let him go."

"Aw, Mary, I can't. Jack will die. Those ba—"

"Kenneth Clark, don't you go using that type of language. Wait until the priest catches up with ya."

Her brother mumbled an apology, but she saw his hold on Jack tighten. She wished there was a way they could keep the pet, but she might as well have wished for a fairy godmother. Their ma wasn't known for her kindness. In fact, the dog might be in more danger at their home than if they left Jack on the streets.

"Kenny love, you know Ma won't let you keep him."

"I hate her. Why does she have to be so awful? Mrs. Fleming was kind, and God took her away. Why couldn't he have taken Ma and left Mrs. Fleming?"

CHAPTER 6

Shocked by her little brother's outburst, Mary didn't know what to say. She couldn't reprimand him for his lack of respect for their mother, as, in fairness, the woman they called Ma didn't deserve respect or anything else. All she cared about was what was in the bottle or pail she sometimes sent Kenny to collect from the bar. Mary pulled her shawl tighter. They needed to get home, not just because of the cold, but if her ma didn't have dinner, the booze would have an even worse effect.

"Come on, Kenny, we got to get back. We are late already."

"I ain't leaving Jack here."

"You can't bring him with you."

"I can. I'll hide him. She won't find him. Please, Mary. Don't make me leave him here. He will die in the snow."

Mary knew she should have insisted, but she could never say no to Kenny, especially now with his tears making two tracks down his dirt-covered face. The blood had started dripping again from the cut on his forehead. Jack whimpered, too, as if to ask could he please come. She laughed at the expression on the puppy's face and found herself saying yes. She didn't want to think of the price she would pay when her ma found out. Nothing ever stayed hidden from Ma for long.

Kenny carried the puppy close to his chest as they trudged along the alleyways until they got to their building. Mary kept an eye out for their mother, but she was nowhere to be seen. Did that mean she was still in bed, or had she gone out already?

She kept Kenny behind her, shielding him, as they walked into their room. The fire was almost out, so she rushed to put more kindling on top. Their room was almost colder than it had been outside. There was no sign of their ma. Mary kept her shawl on as she rummaged through the dresser for some food. She had left bread and a small hunk of cheese there that morning, but it was gone. There was nothing for them to eat.

"I'm starvin', and so is Jack. When's dinner?" Kenny whined, as he sat almost on top of the pitiful, small fire.

"How about I treat us both to a bowl of soup from old Murphy's stall? Maybe he might have a small bone for Jack?"

Kenny threw himself at her, grabbing her by the legs, almost making her fall over.

"You're the best sister ever, Mary."

She hugged him back, wishing that were true. If she had been a good sister, she would have found a way to protect Kenny. He was so thin his clothes, such as they were, just hung on him. Mrs. Fleming used to joke, he was a gannet, always starving. But, since she'd died last year, things had been even worse for her brother. She went to find her hidden pile of coins. Her ma didn't know about this money, or else she would have spent it. She insisted Mary give up all her wages, but the foreman had given her some extra pennies for getting a job done earlier than expected. It was these she would use for her brother's dinner.

"First, we need to clean you up."

"Ah, Mary do you have to? I hate being washed."

"Yes, I do. We don't want the neighbors talking about ya. Do you want Ma to know you were fightin'?"

Kenny shook his head. He didn't complain, even when she washed the cut on his head. She didn't have anything to cover it with. The air would help it heal faster.

"Can we go now? Me belly hurts."

"Yes, Kenny. Just let me get rid of this." Mary threw out the blood-stained water and hid the evidence of her brother's mishap. Their ma didn't need an excuse to beat Kenny, so it was best she didn't find out about the fight.

CHAPTER 7

athleen Collins sat by the fire in Lily's house, her sister Bridget beside her. Lily sat on a chair on the other side of the large fire. Richard, Carl, and Charlie were in Charlie's office discussing business. Kathleen was thrilled Richard got on so well with her friends.

"Richard seems to be progressing well with his studies. Charlie says his reputation is growing," Bridget commented.

Bridget and Carl were staying with Lily and Charlie, as was their habit when they came to New York. Their fears for how

Bridget would react to Laurie and Teddy, Lily's twin boys, were unfounded. Bridget adored both of them and insisted on being their main caregiver so Lily could rest more during the final stages of her pregnancy. Kathleen was struck again by how unfair life could be as she watched her sister with the babies, which proved what a wonderful mother Bridget would have made.

"Richard has operated on quite a few rich people now, so he's hoping news of his talent will spread. He still wants to set up a clinic near the sanctuary so he can spend a couple of days a week helping the poor. They could never afford to see a plastic surgeon. Most of them don't even call the doctor when they are ill," Kathleen replied, staring deep into the fire. "I don't think his work during the cholera outbreak won him any friends though. Not among those rich people. They didn't seem to understand his need to be among the poor."

"Don't judge them too harshly, Kathleen. People are afraid of cholera. Most doctors know how easily it spreads, and they didn't want a repeat of what happened back in '92," Bridget admonished gently before surprising her by saying, "Richard and you are well suited."

She looked at her sister in shock, having assumed she would be concerned about the age gap.

"You don't think he is too old for me?" Kathleen asked Bridget, who was looking at Lily with concern, as Lily moved in her seat. She was huge in her advanced state of pregnancy.

"From what Bridget says, you were born old," Lily teased her, as Bridget nodded while smiling. "Shane likes him, too."

Kathleen wasn't sure she wanted to talk about her brother. She had thought the young man would have learned his lesson, but since coming back to New York, he had gotten mixed up with the old gangs from the neighborhood. He seemed to spend a lot of time down in Hell's Kitchen. Lily told her often Shane was just working through his experiences and would be fine in time, but Kathleen wasn't too sure. She didn't see her brother as much as she should, but on the rare occasions he showed up at the sanctuary, he always looked half-starved and showed signs of bruising. He hadn't looked much better yesterday when he arrived at Lily's house to say hello to Bridget and Carl. Lily had invited him to stay, saying she had plenty of space, but Shane had declined. He didn't stay long, saying he had business to take care of. Nobody had asked what type of business.

"Kathleen, stop screwing up your face. You look like you sucked on a whole bag of lemon drops. Who are you thinking about? Shane or Maura?" Bridget asked.

"How did you know?" Even as she asked, Kathleen knew the answer. Bridget had always been able to read her mind.

"With Christmas coming up, it's only natural your thoughts would be on our family. What about Michael? Has he written back to you yet?" Bridget asked.

Kathleen shook her head. She had written to her brother every month since finding him. In the last fifteen months, she had two replies, the first a letter for last year's Christmas and the second a note on her birthday. This year she had sent him a parcel for Christmas with some new clothes, warm socks, and underthings, as well as a couple of books. She didn't know if he would get the gifts or not, even though she had included a note for the prison guards with a small gift for them. She hoped Michael had gotten them. The weather was viciously cold, and no doubt the prison was even worse than usual.

"What is the latest on Maura?" Lily asked, as she slipped off her shoes. Kathleen noted her friend's swollen feet and pulled up a stool for Lily to rest them on.

"Tommy and Mini Mike found out a little about the man she and the others ran off with. None of it was good news, and we haven't heard anything else. Neither of them thinks we will see Maura again."

Bridget's lips thinned. Kathleen knew she hadn't forgiven Maura for what she had done. Bella had been lucky to walk away with a minor head injury, not that Maura had stopped to check on their friend after her new man friend had knocked Bella out.

"Oh, Kathleen, Bridget, I am so sorry. I know what she did was wrong, but she is still your sister."

Kathleen didn't want to talk about Maura but wasn't sure how to change the subject. Thankfully, the door opened, and the men walked in.

"Are you ready to go, Kathleen? I can escort you home before heading back to the hospital," Richard asked, after he greeted Lily and Bridget.

"This late?" she said standing up.

"Yes, I have a patient I want to check up on. The operation went as well as could be expected, but I can't help thinking I missed something. I won't sleep without seeing her again."

"You're so dedicated, Richard. Your patients are lucky to have you."

"Thank you, Lily, but I believe the work you do at the sanctuary is far more important."

Kathleen kissed Lily on the cheek before reminding her friend to join them in the sanctuary on Friday evening for the Christmas tree decorating. Bridget had told her she would be there as much as possible in the intervening week to help out.

"We wouldn't miss it, would we Charlie? It is such a delight to see their little faces light up with excitement."

"Yes, they are so excited. Some of the girls have been sewing decorations and have persuaded the boys to join in. It will be fun. You should bring the babies, too." Kathleen suggested, as she took her coat from Charlie's hand. She kissed Bridget and Lily goodbye and gave Carl a hug. She adored her brother-in-law, who had made Bridget so happy.

"We will. Safe home, and see you on Friday," Charlie called from his door, as Richard escorted her to the waiting cab. She shivered as much from the cold as the slight touch of his hand on her arm.

"I'm sorry I didn't get much time to spend with you tonight," Richard apologized, once they got settled in the cab.

"Don't be. I love how well you and Charlie get on. Does he think your quest for funding will work?"

Richard was trying to raise money to fund more research into burn treatments, specifically for children, but at a time when the economy was suffering, it was proving difficult. Charlie had some contacts who Richard hoped would help.

"Yes, Charlie thinks he can drum up some interest. We may have our clinic before too long."

Our clinic? Did he mean his and hers or was that his way of talking in general? Was this the moment to tell him she loved him?

Her chance passed as he spoke again.

"The snow is falling pretty heavy tonight."

They turned down the street toward the sanctuary.

"Yes, it will be freezing for all those without shelter. I love Christmas, Richard, but I wish we could provide room and board for all the families that need it."

Richard didn't reply but took her hands and warmed them in his. Then he helped her out of the cab, kissed her on the forehead and waited for her to go inside the sanctuary. Before she had closed the door, he was gone, back out into the snow. She hoped his patient would recover but couldn't help feeling a little bit miffed he had hurried off.

CHAPTER 8

 enny and Mary shivered as they walked quickly to Murphy's stall. He was at the end of the line of stalls, and most of his neighbors had already closed up. The street was covered in the mess they left behind with street urchins digging through the waste in the hope of salvaging some food. Mary held onto Kenny's arm tighter, as they picked their way through the debris to reach Mr. Murphy. The large, red-faced man with the bulbous nose and kind eyes was close to

closing up for the day, but he smiled warmly at the two of them.

"Mary lass, you just caught me before I was off to home. Wow, Kenny lad, that's some bruise you got. Were you fighting again?"

"Yes, Mr. Murphy, but it wasn't my fault. The other lads were bigger than me."

"They always are, son. Bullies never pick on their own size. You run away next time you see them. You don't want them beating you again," Mr. Murphy said.

"Yes, sir."

"Mary, what can I get you?"

"A bowl of soup and a piece of bread for Kenny, please. And an old bone if you have it."

"Sorry, Mary, but I put the bones into the soup. It gives extra nourishment. What did you want a bone for anyway? Growing girl like you needs soup yourself."

"It's for my dog, Mr. Murphy. Mary said she would feed Jack. He's starvin'," Kenny explained.

Murphy's eyes met Mary's, and she hated seeing the pity in the older man's face. She didn't have much pride. She couldn't afford it, but she hated anyone knowing just how badly off they were. In this place, where everyone was struggling to get by, they weren't the only ones starving. But while many families had their men drinking the wages, it was still unusual for a mother to put the gin before her own children.

"I'm not hungry. I ate at work. Kenny hasn't eaten since breakfast," she said bravely, despite the wave of longing hitting her with the smell. She saw by his expression that he didn't believe her.

"Go on, Mary, have a cup of soup. You'll be doing me a favor. I want to go home to the missus, but I can't until the urn is empty. And I won't waste good food. Go on now, child, get that into ya. I have a piece of stale bread, too—if you dunk it into the soup, it will be fine. I won't charge you for it. Sure, the birds would have benefited from it, if you two hadn't come along."

Mary accepted the gift gratefully, knowing full well Mr. Murphy was being kind. He had a family of his own to feed, and she was certain Mrs. Murphy would have found a use for both the leftover bread and soup.

It was delicious, but then hunger was a good appetizer, Da had said. A tear escaped, as she thought of her dad. Why had he left them? Couldn't he have taken them with him when he went?

"Here, lad, give that to your dog. Just watch he doesn't choke."

"Mary, look at what Jack got. Thanks, Mr. Murphy, you is the best."

Mary could see the old man was embarrassed by her brother's outburst. He packed up his stall in record time.

"You children should get home now. Nasty storm coming, my bones are playing me up, always do when snow is on the way."

"Thank you, Mr. Murphy. We will go inside now. Come on, Kenny. Ma will be waiting."

"Will she be back? Do you think she went shopping, Mary?"

Mortified she had even mentioned their mother, Mary didn't answer but hurried Kenny and his dog back in the direction of their home. Relieved to find her ma hadn't come home yet, she warned Kenny not to mention buying soup for dinner. Then she gave his face another quick wash to stop the cut going bad and put him to bed.

She woke sometime later, the cold seeping into her bones. There was no sign of her ma. She risked putting some more wood on the fire. Her ma would be mad, but she was freezing. Then she climbed into bed, wishing the newspapers she used for bedding were real bedclothes. Shivering, she finally fell asleep.

CHAPTER 9

*N*ext morning, she woke early, but there was still no sign of their ma. She would have to bring Kenny to work. Her boss would not be pleased, but she couldn't leave him in their room all day alone.

The young boy moaned and whined the whole way to the factory where Mary worked. Once there, one of the seamstresses took pity on him and hid him in a store cupboard, giving him a sandwich and an apple. Kenny thought Christmas had come early.

Mary put her head down and started sewing. Where was her ma, and would she come back? Mary wasn't at all sure she wanted her to and immediately felt guilty at even thinking that thought.

THE FINAL WHISTLE BLEW, allowing Mary to go find Kenny. He was asleep in the corner of the store cupboard. Wiping his eyes, he came quietly when she motioned him it was time to go home.

They trudged through the snow, thankful for once the smell of horse drop-pings and other rubbish had been masked by the snow. Kenny's little hand was frozen. No doubt he had lost his gloves in the fight. She had knitted them from an old jumper of their dad's. A lump appeared in her throat just thinking of their dad. He had been a big, handsome man. Black Jack Clark they had called him around here, on account of his being from Galway, Ireland.

She remembered him laughing. He did that often, especially after a few drinks. He and Ma had been happy once, but that was before their da had lost his job in the crash. The fights had started soon after. She'd climb into Kenny's bed and hold her little brother tight, as their ma and da got into yet another argument. Da hit ma, but then she hit him back just as hard. His head broke more than his fair share of cooking pots. Then baby Joseph had died, and that was that. Da went out one day and never came back. Nobody knew where he'd gone. Some said he'd gone back to Ireland, but they were just guessing. Ma had cried for weeks, but now she wouldn't hear mention of their da again. She said he was dead to her and them.

CHAPTER 10

*M*onday morning dawned bright and early, a weak sun fighting to rise in the sky. Kathleen looked out the window at the picture perfect view. The snow was like a white blanket covering everything. It looked beautiful, but she knew it wouldn't last. It would soon turn black, as people came and went. She spotted an ambulance making its way down the street outside, the poor horse looked frozen. She sent up a quick prayer for the passenger, before turning her attention on the day ahead.

She had spoken to Bridget briefly at mass the day before, and her sister had promised to be at the sanctuary early. Carl was going to stay at Lily's house with Teddy and Laurie. Lily felt it was too cold for the twins to leave their home, but Kathleen guessed she was also a little worried they may catch a cold or worse from the crowd at the sanctuary. The children were getting excited, counting down the days until Santa would come to visit them.

As she stared out the window, she couldn't help but think of the children on the streets. If only there was a way to give them a happy Christmas. Given the weather, they would be struggling to survive the cold, and food was likely to be scarce as people would stay indoors where possible. She should speak to Bridget about taking some food baskets to Mr. Fleming and other families in their old neighborhood. Feeling a bit chilly, she washed and dressed quickly before going downstairs to the kitchen where Cook was already working over the hot stove. Her cheeks were rosy red, as she turned to say good morning.

"Cook, have we enough coal and wood to see us through?" Kathleen asked. "I meant to check with you before but got distracted."

"Tommy and Mini Mike brought us loads, Miss Kathleen, so don't you fret. We have enough to heat the whole of New York. Doesn't it feel chilly this morning? I made hot cocoa for the children. Would you like some?"

Kathleen grinned. Cook knew her penchant for cocoa. She loved the rich taste and suspected Cook added her own special twist.

"Will Miss Bridget be here soon?" Cook asked, as she sat at the table, a steaming cup of tea in front of her.

"Yes, I am expecting her any minute. She said she would be around a lot over the next few weeks. Carl and she will be taking the children on the train in early January, depending, of course, on good weather. We could be snowed in, judging by this lot."

"Don't be saying things like that, Miss Kathleen. I've had enough snow to last me a lifetime. I can't wait for summer."

"Don't you like Christmas?" Kathleen asked, curiosity getting the better of her. She never asked Cook about her family, having been told it was something she didn't like to talk about.

"I like Christmas day. I love going to mass and then seeing the children's faces, as they open their presents, but it's only one day. The rest of winter is miserable. I know we're lucky here, as we have warm shelter and lots of good food, but it wasn't always like that. I can remember going to bed cold, hungry, and terrified."

"You were scared?" Kathleen couldn't help asking. The idea of the kind, old woman being scared of anything didn't seem right.

"I was, out of my wits. You see, where I lived back in Ireland was in the middle of the so-called rebel country. The English would raid our home over and over looking for people. They took my daddy away and then my brothers, didn't care they were innocent. Daddy might have given the rebels shelter and the odd meal, but he wasn't personally involved. But that didn't help him at the trial. They didn't care my brothers were underage either. They sent them all to prison in England." Cook took out a large hanky and blew her nose noisily before continuing, "Mam had a brother in America, and he sent home money for our passage. She stayed in Ireland but sent my sister and me over here. My sister got married and went west, and I became a maid in a big house. I was lucky. The people were good to me, and the cook was a grand lady. She taught me everything I know, and so here I am."

Cook seemed embarrassed to have been talking for so long. Kathleen was quick to reassure her.

"You lived an eventful life, Cook. And I

am sorry for what happened to your father and brothers. But I am glad you ended up with us. I don't know what we would do without you here in the sanctuary."

"Ah, go on, Miss Kathleen. I don't do anything special."

"But you do, Cook. You make wonderful meals for us, sometimes out of very little, when supplies run low. You helped the children get better when they fell ill. Your chicken soup could cure a lot of people. Maybe you should can it and sell it?"

"Miss Kathleen, you get some wild ideas sometimes. Whoever heard of canned soup? Now I best get on. We are going to make sure our children have the best Christmas. Drink up that cocoa, before it gets cold."

Cook stood and busied herself with her work, but Kathleen knew her comments had delighted the older woman. She should speak to Lily and Bridget to ask for their help in finding the perfect present for Cook. She wanted everyone to have something under the tree waiting to be opened on Christmas day.

"Says here in the paper the President is going to have a tree with electric lights in the White House. Can you imagine that?" Kathleen asked.

"Electric lights?" Cook balked. "They are going to burn down that house and maybe take him with them. What sort of things goes through people's heads?"

"I think it might be safer than candles, but who knows. We have to make sure the children know the lights get blown out every night. We can't risk a fire at the sanctuary," Kathleen mused aloud as she continued reading the paper while drinking her cocoa.

Soon the excited murmurs of children's voices alerted her to how much time had passed. She had more than a full day's work ahead of her.

"Thank you, Cook. That was just what the doctor ordered."

"Hmph. I hope that doctor of yours orders you something a lot nicer than a hot cocoa, Kathleen."

Kathleen ran, wishing she hadn't mentioned doctors. Now Cook would be teasing her as well.

CHAPTER 11

It had been a long day at the factory. The boss had made her work an extra hour unpaid. He said it was to pay for the shelter he provided for Kenny. Their ma hadn't arrived back after the weekend, and she had no option but to take him to work with her again. She was so tired she could have fallen asleep on her feet.

As they neared their home, they heard their ma screaming. She was fighting with one of the new neighbors. Mary thought the family was Italian, but she wasn't sure.

It was unusual for a non-Irish family to move into their tenements, but she guessed the new families couldn't afford to be choosy. Kenny shrank back closer to her. She took his hand and pulled him under the long streamers of garments fluttering from the fire escapes. Despite the cold, frosty weather, some of the women insisted on hanging out their laundry. They waited to see if the argument would stop, but her ma seemed to be getting more heated by the minute. Mary's eyes darted around looking for an escape. She spotted Granny Belbin who motioned for them to come closer.

"Come in here, dearie, and bring the little fella with you. I have some warm tea in the pot. Can't give you nuffink much for your bellies, but at least you won't be stood out in the cold."

"Thank you, Granny Belbin," Mary responded, dragging Kenny in behind her. Her brother, like most of the children from the tenement, was scared of Granny Belbin. She was really old and looked like one of the characters in the Macy's Christmas store window. She was a stern old lady who didn't stand much nonsense, but Mary knew her gruff exterior hid a warm heart. Granny Belbin had sheltered Mary more than once when one of her ma's male friends had taken an interest in her.

"Come on, Kenny, Granny Belbin won't bite ya," Mary said.

"I might, but I don't have me teeth," Granny teased, making Kenny blanch. He was now almost glued to Mary's side, still clutching his precious bundle.

"What you got there, young Kenny?" Granny Belbin asked, as they made themselves comfortable in her little room. Although it was small, it was spotless, or at least as close to spotless as any of the tenement hovels could be.

"Nuffink," Kenny answered, not looking up from the floor.

"Well, the nuffink sure is wriggling. Maybe he or she wants to get down to the floor." Granny winked at Mary. "Do you have a black cat under there? I can't find Myrtle. She ran away a week ago now and still hasn't come home. I got to have my black cat, or my spells don't work."

Mary hid a smile as Kenny stared at Granny, his mouth hanging open. The child had completely forgotten the scene outside with their ma.

"You really are a witch?" Kenny asked, slowly.

"Na lad, I is just an old lady. Now put down your bundle and get some hot tea into ya. You look like you were in the wars."

"Kenny was fighting last week," Mary's explanation was interrupted by her brother.

"I had to save Jack. They was going to kill him. I couldn't let them do that, although Ma is going to kill him, when she sees him."

"She'd be lucky to see her own feet, the state she's in today. Sorry, Mary. I shouldn't say bad things about your ma, but the state of her. She's been mouthin' off all afternoon. It's a wonder someone hasn't had the coppers down here."

"What upset her this time? Do you know?"

"No idea, love. She accused the new widow, a nice young lady with beautiful manners, of stealing something. Sure, what would Rosa Italian want with anything be-longing to your ma?"

"Is that her name? I saw her a couple of times over the weekend. She is so beautiful, isn't she? And her baby, he is so handsome with his big, brown eyes."

CHAPTER 12

Granny laughed as she handed Kenny a cookie. His eyes widened, but before he took a bite, he broke the cookie into four pieces. He gave one to Mary, handed one to Granny, and then shared the other two between Jack and himself.

"Her name's not Rosa. I have no idea what she is called or why she is here, as she hasn't spoken to any of us. I don't think she can speak English, but maybe that's a good thing. She won't last long around here. She needs to move up to her own people in the Italian quarter."

"Why does it have to be like that, Granny? Irish here, Italians there, and someone else over the river?"

"Just the way it is girl. Helps stop trouble."

As if their ma heard Granny, her screams escalated. Granny exchanged a look with Mary, before they both laughed. Kenny looked bewildered.

"Your mam's been hitting the liquor hard all day, Mary," Granny whispered to her, as Kenny lay on the floor playing with Jack. "I think its best if you both stayed here tonight."

"I can't, Granny. If you can, keep Kenny, please, but I got to check on Ma. She's all we got."

Granny didn't reply, but her pursed lips said everything. Mary knew she was taking a risk going upstairs to their home, but she wouldn't be able to live with the guilt if her ma hurt herself. She had hit her head one time, and another she had been ill and not woken up. She needed her.

"Mary, I want to stay with you. I don't want to be alone." Kenny scooped Jack up in his arms and inched closer to Mary.

"You won't be alone, Kenny. Granny will look after you," Mary said firmly, despite the begging look on her brother's face. He was not safe with her ma. When drunk, she blamed the boy for her husband leaving, as if Dad had left because of his son.

"Kenny, you and Jack make a bed over there by the fire. You will be warm," Granny insisted. "Mary will be back before you know it."

Mary gave Granny a grateful look before giving Kenny a hug. "You behave for Granny now, and I will see you first thing in the morning."

"You really mean it? You will let Jack stay here?" Kenny asked Granny.

"You need to take him out for a walk and make sure he does his business. If he makes a mess in here, you will clean it up, but I like dogs. Not that he is much to look at, not at the moment, but he will grow into a fine ratter, I guess. Won't you, Jack?"

Mary grinned as the dog wagged its tail. Somebody knew which side his bread was buttered on.

She left the little group and headed slowly up the stairs. The screeching had stopped, which only meant one thing. Her ma had passed out. She felt in her pocket for her key, not that she ever had to use it. Ma always left the door open.

She pushed inside, relieved to see her ma had managed to make it onto the bed. She wouldn't have to pick her up. She crept closer and saw her ma appeared to be sleeping. As she turned away, a hand grabbed her leg, scaring the daylights out of her.

"Mary, is that you?"

"Yes, Ma."

"Youse late. What took you so long? Wha' his name?"

"Who Ma?"

Her ma staggered up to a sitting position and glared at her. "Don't you back answer me girl. I know what's you be up to. The whole neighborhood has been talkin' about ya."

"Ma, I haven't been doing anything. I went to work, and I came home. Are you hungry? Do you want me to cook your dinner?" There was some oatmeal hidden in the cupboard for Kenny's breakfast.

"You mark my words, Mary. He don't want you for nuthin' but his wicked way. You'll see."

"Ma, lie down and let me make you something to eat, please."

Her ma lay back down without argument. She was so surprised, she stared at her mother for a few minutes before turning away. Then she heard the sobs.

"Ma, what is it? Why are you crying?" Seeing her mother so upset was unnerving. She could handle it when her ma was screaming or throwing punches, but crying? Her ma never cried.

"I saw him today, so I did. Your da. There he was, bold as brass with that Italian hussy from across the hall. She thinks she can hide him from me. Me own husband. So, help me, God, but I is still married to the old sod."

"Ma, shush. Don't cry. You can't have seen Da. He left months ago. Remember?"

"No, Mary. He's come back. He's here, I'm telling ya." Her ma became more agitated, as she struggled to sit upright.

"Okay, Ma. Why don't you try to rest now, and, when you wake up, we can go find him together?"

"You're a good girl, Mary. Do you know that?"

Mary didn't reply as her ma's eyes closed. Jesus, Mary, and Joseph, she prayed, her ma had lost her reason. What was she going to do now?

CHAPTER 13

Her ma had a fitful night's sleep, but thankfully, she didn't start ranting or raving again. She was snoring heavily when Mary let herself out to work. She brought some breakfast down to Granny and Kenny. She wasn't sure what the old lady did for money, but nobody could afford to be feeding someone else's child for long. Not these days. Granny accepted the oatmeal gratefully, promised Kenny could stay with her all day, and said she would see Mary later. Mary didn't want to leave her brother, but she had to get to work. There were plenty of girls willing and able to step into her shoes at the cuff and collar factory, where she worked six and a half days a week. Her nose tingled by the time she got to work, and her fingers were numb. It was awful cold, but thankfully not yet snowing. And the sun was out, which brought a smile to at least a few people's faces.

"Fine morning, isn't it, Mary?"

She liked Mr. Fleming, the man who greeted her. His wife had been very kind to both Kenny and her. She had been a lovely woman.

"It is indeed, Mr. Fleming. How are your girls?"

"Fine, thank you, love. Missing their ma but so aren't we all. Best get going, love, as the whistle will blow any minute. Don't want to be locked out, do we?"

Mary hadn't realized the time. She walked faster. The last thing she needed was to miss a day's wages. She earned little enough as it was. She arrived just in time as the floor manager spotted her and held the gate.

"You're cutting it fine today, Mary."

"Sorry, sir, my ma wasn't feeling too well this morning."

She didn't wait for a reply. She headed to her desk intent on getting her work done. She had a bonus to reach and that meant getting more cuffs finished than she had done yesterday.

"MARY, are you ready to go home? The final whistle blew five minutes ago."

Mary glanced up to see her friend Breda waiting for her.

"Sorry, I was miles away. Just coming." She tidied up around her desk and grabbed her shawl.

"It's brass monkey weather out there. The snow will be six feet deep if it keeps up at this rate," Breda said.

"It's snowing? Kenny will love that. He likes making snowmen," Mary replied.

"Boys will be boys. I can't bear it meself. Never could. Ma says I was always to be found on top of the fire. She said I was lucky I didn't get my backside fried."

Mary laughed despite her friend's coarse words. Breda came from a large but loving family. She'd lost count how many brothers and sisters Breda had. She'd only met her ma once but had been left with a lasting impression of a lady with a nice, rounded face and big brown eyes full of laughter. She wondered if her own ma had ever laughed. Not for a long time, that was for sure.

"You all right, Mary?"

"Just thinking about what to make for dinner," Mary lied quickly. She hated lying, but she wasn't about to tell Breda she was wondering what state her ma would be in when she got home. With any luck, she wouldn't be raving about Mary's da.

CHAPTER 14

When she got home, all was quiet. She peeped into granny's, but there was no sign of the old lady or Kenny. No sign of Jack either. She went upstairs and found her ma sitting by an unlit fire, staring into space.

"Evening, Ma. It's awful cold out. Do you want me to light the fire for ya?"

No response.

"Ma? Did you hear me?"

Her ma turned on her, eyes wide with hatred, her red face turning purple as her temper exploded.

"Don't you come in here acting all innocent. I know what you been up to my girl. You're a harlot. Get out of my house. I never want to see you again. Do you hear me?"

"Ma? What are you talking about? I don't even know what that name means?" She didn't either, although she knew it wasn't a compliment.

"I been hearing stories about you all day. They been telling me."

Scared now, Mary backed up toward the door. "Ma, there's nobody here. Who you been talking to?"

"Them? Don't you pretend you can't see them? They are all around you. You can hear them, too. They is calling you names, Mary Ann Elizabeth Clark. They know what you is, a Jezebel. Well, I know what to do about you. I was told…"

Too late Mary saw the poker in her ma's hand. She held up her hands to defend herself, but her ma's strength was overpowering. Over and over her ma hit her, the pain so excruciating, until finally, she felt it no more.

CHAPTER 15

Kenny walked back and forth across Granny's small hovel. "You'd wear a hole in the carpet if I had one. Mary will be here when she is ready. We just got to be patient."

"She should have been here long ago, Granny. She's never been this late. Something happened to her. I know it."

"Shush child. You know nothin'. You need to take Jack out for a walk. Don't want him messin' up my floor again."

"He didn't mean to do it, Granny. He's just a puppy. He's learnin'. You won't beat him, will you? Promise me you won't. You can hit me instead."

"Hush, child. I ain't beating anyone, not you or your pet. You poor unfortunate boy, to believe I could do that to a fine boy like yourself. Why, if I was only forty years younger, I would pack Mary and you up and run off with ye. Away from that bowser you call a mother. She isn't fit to have ye. Do you hear me?"

"You's shoutin', Granny. You're scaring Jack." In reality, Jack seemed just fine sitting at Granny's feet in front of the fire, but Kenny was terrified. Granny hated his ma. That wasn't really a shock. Nobody he knew liked his ma, but she was still his mother. She was all he had, apart from Mary. Mary was grand for a big sister. A bit bossy and she had a way of knowing what he was up to and when he was lying, but she was a good sort. But he didn't want nobody taking him away from his ma. They were his family.

"Granny, maybe I should go up and

check with Ma to see if she has seen Mary?" Kenny asked.

"I don't think that's a good idea, pet. Mary will come down when she can."

"But it's been hours, and I can't go to sleep until I knows she is okay. Maybe she got stuck in the snow."

"Hardly child. There's barely enough out there to build a snowman. Not like the blizzard of '88. That was something else, believe me. The stories I could tell ya…"

And Granny was off. He found her stories interesting now that he wasn't afraid of her no more, but he didn't want to listen to them now. He wanted to see his ma and Mary. He missed them, both of them. Maybe Granny would nod off, and he could sneak upstairs. That's what he would do. He would pretend to listen to her stories and then sneak out when her eyes closed.

He lay down to listen, as Granny told him about the blizzard bringing snow so deep it covered right up to the church roof.

CHAPTER 16

He woke to Jack sniffing and licking his face, making a funny crying sound. "What's the matter, boy?"

Jack kept moving toward the door and coming back to him. "You want me to come outside? Now? It's freezing. You got to go? Man, do you pick your times."

Kenny grumbled as he stood up. Granny was snoring softly by the fire. He tiptoed past her and opened the door, but instead of going downstairs, Jack bolted upstairs.

"Where are you going? Come back here,

you bad dog. You is going to get me into trouble. Knew I shouldn't have shown you where we lived. If Ma catches you, you will be made into sausages. Come back, I tell you. Come back."

The dog didn't listen but instead stopped just briefly at the door and pushed it open. Ma hadn't locked it. He followed inside as Jack began to bark. His barks were loud enough to wake the dead. Kenny pushed the door open farther, as it was dark. Where were the matches? He didn't like the dark. It scared him. The fire wasn't lit, but he fumbled around until he found a match. Then he lit a candle, even though he knew he would be in trouble for that, too. Still, if his ma didn't kill him for having a dog in her house, she wasn't going to worry about the candle, was she?

He turned back, and what he saw nearly scared him out of his wits. Mary was lying on the floor, a puddle of something wet beside her.

"Ma, come quick. Mary's hurt. Mary,

wake up, it's Kenny. Mary, please wake up.
Mary." But Mary wouldn't wake up. She
didn't move. Jack whined and kept pawing
at her face, but her eyes didn't open. Kenny
tried to move her face, but it was all wet.

"Jack, get Granny. Fetch Granny." He
didn't know if the dog knew what he
meant, but Jack ran off, leaving him alone.
He held the candle up to check his ma's bed,
but it was empty. She wasn't there. Where
was she?

Water. He had to get water to wash
Mary's face. He picked the candle up and
walked over to the jug. The candle cast
funny shadows on the wall. It was creepy,
and he wished someone would come. He
didn't like it just being the two of them, not
when Mary was so silent.

"Kenny Clark, your dog will be the—Oh,
Mary mother of Jesus, what happened here?
Go fetch Mr. Fleming, lad. Now. Go on."

CHAPTER 17

*G*ranny almost pushed him out of the door. He knew where the Flemings lived. Mrs. Fleming had fed him cakes sometimes. She'd been a nice lady before she died. He ran down two flights of stairs and found their door. Banging heavily, he shouted for Mr. Fleming to come quick. Some neighbors opened their doors to curse at him, but he didn't pay any attention. The Flemings' door opened, Mr. Fleming coming out as he pulled up his suspenders.

"Kenny, what is it? Do you know what time it is?"

"Sorry, Mr. Fleming. Granny sent me to get ya. Ma is gone, and Mary, she's asleep on the floor. Only she won't wake up. She spilled something too, as it's all over the floor. See?" He held up his hand, only then seeing it was red. The floor moved quickly, as he staggered. His hand had blood on it. It had to be...

"Lad. Stay here with my girls. Jessica, watch over him. There's something wrong at home. Keep him here. And wash his hands, for goodness' sake."

Kenny didn't argue. He seemed to have lost the ability to speak. Jessica wrapped her arm around his shoulders, and he didn't shrug it off, even though she was an annoying girl. He let her lead him into their house as her father ran back up the stairs. Jessica washed his hands and his face. It was then he remembered Jack. He had to find his dog, as he would be frightened. He asked Jessica for a drink of water, and as soon as she was distracted, he bolted out of the door and ran all the way to his place. He stopped at the door at the sight in front of him. There was plenty of light now. He could see Mary lying on his ma's bed, her face paler than the pillow. There was a man there who was looking at her head. Granny, Mr. Fleming, and some other people were huddled in one corner, but it was the policeman holding his dog he recognized. Jack jumped out of the man's arms as soon as he spotted Kenny. What was Inspector Griffith doing here? He never came to the tenements, not in the middle of the night, but was it still nighttime, when all these people were still around?

CHAPTER 18

*W*heels rattled over the cobblestones outside. Children screamed, and mothers ranted, but there wasn't a sound in the room. Everyone seemed to be staring at him. He bent down to pick Jack up. The dog licked his face, as he held it even closer.

"Mary?" he said.

"Child, you shouldn't be here. Didn't Mr. Fleming tell you to stay with his Jessica?"

"Yes, Granny, but I had to come and find Jack, Mary, and Ma. They is my family."

"They were, son, that they were. God loves you now, more than ever." Granny crossed herself, as she spoke.

Kenny didn't know why God would love him now more than before. He hadn't done anything particularly nice. If anything, he should be in trouble, as he had hidden Jack from his ma. That wasn't a good thing to do, as he had disobeyed her. The priest would give him penance in confession, if he went.

"Who is that man with Mary, and why is Inspector Griffin here?" he asked.

"You know Inspector Griffin?" Granny asked, her eyebrows raised.

"Yes, he came to our school. He was talking about gangs. Least I think he was talking about them. I wasn't really paying attention. He had a big, black dog with him. He said it was a police dog. He let me play with it."

"That I did, lad, and you were wonderful with Duke. He's a grand, old dog. Retired now. So, Kenny, tell me where you think your ma is?"

"Ma? Isn't she here? She should be here. It's nearly morning time. She don't stay out all night. Not often."

He saw the adults look at each other, but he didn't know what that look meant. He glanced toward Mary, but the man wasn't looking at his sister anymore. He was looking at Kenny. He didn't like them all looking at him.

"Why are you all staring at me? When is Mary going to wake up? She'll be in trouble if she is late for work. They don't like that. She told me."

"Listen, lad, I got something to tell you. You know Mary had an accident—"

Kenny interrupted the policeman, "Accident?"

Kenny pulled Jack tighter to his chest. Granny had moved closer and put her arm around his shoulders. She was sniffing, as if she were crying.

"What do you mean?"

"Kenny, you will have to be brave," Granny said. "Mary was hurt last night, and, well son, I am afraid she isn't going to wake up."

"Mary? Who'd hurt Mary?" he asked. Everyone liked Mary. She was sweet and kind and funny. Even if she was bossy, but that was only cause she loved him.

"Why can't you make Mary wake up? Throw some water in her face. We used to do that to Ma sometimes, but you have to stand back, or she will hit you."

"Oh, Kenny. The things you have seen, and you is not yet six years old." Granny held him tighter. It was hard to breathe, not just because she was squeezing him, but she didn't smell too good.

CHAPTER 19

"Kenny, did you see your ma yesterday? It's very important to tell me the truth." Inspector Griffin had his cross face on. Kenny kicked at the floor. Should he lie? Or should he tell the policeman he had come up looking for his ma during the day when Granny was asleep? He wasn't supposed to, but he had wanted to see her. Only she'd been in bed fast asleep. She hadn't even woken up when Jack had barked, trying to say hello. He had been so scared, thinking she was going to jump out of the bed and throw

Jack out the window, but she hadn't even moved.

"Kenny, tell me. Did you see her yesterday?"

Kenny nodded.

"When lad? You are not in trouble. We know you haven't done anything wrong."

"I came up yesterday when Granny fell asleep. I wanted to see her. I missed her. I know she shouts a lot and hits Mary and me, but she's my ma. I love her. So, I crept up to see her and brought Jack. He barked, but she didn't wake up, not properly. She turned around in the bed and made this sound." He snorted for the policeman, thinking he had done a good job of imitating his mother. But Inspector Griffin didn't laugh.

"I ran back down to Granny's. I didn't want her to know I had gone out without asking, and I didn't want Ma to wake up. Mary wasn't home then, as it wasn't late."

"How did you know to come up and find Mary?"

"I didn't. I was going to sneak out again, but Granny started telling me stories about the blizzard, and I guess I fell asleep. She did, too, as she was snoring when I woke up. Jack licked my face and then ran to the door. I thought he needed to … you know … go," Kenny mumbled, embarrassed as all the adults continued to stare at him.

"What happened then?"

"Jack came running up here. I thought he was going to wake Ma, and I ran after him to stop him. The door was open, and he came in and started licking Mary's face, but she wouldn't wake up. I knelt down beside her. The ground was wet. But I couldn't wake her either, and ma's bed was empty. Then Jack went for Granny, and … well, I guess you know the rest."

Kenny fought to keep the tears back as his voice got all croaky. He couldn't cry. His ma always said real men didn't cry, and he was a man, wasn't he? He held Jack so tight the dog whimpered and licked his face. He buried his face into the dog, not wanting anyone to see his tears.

"Kenny lad, you come with me now. I am going to get you some breakfast and some new clothes. Inspector Griffin, I will have him until you find someone."

"Thanks, Granny Belbin. I will be back later today. I best get the wagon over here and let the priest know. Were they part of Father Nelson's church, do you know? I can't remember seeing them at mass."

"They didn't go often, I don't think. Mary tried, but the poor girl was run ragged having to look after her ma and the boy."

"Father Nelson is nice. He came to school one time. But Father Drayton is our priest. He scares me. Mary didn't like him either. Said he made her feel funny. You won't leave her alone with him, will you? She'll be scared. She didn't like being alone."

"No, son, I won't. Now you don't worry about a thing. Go with Granny."

"But, Inspector?"

"Yes, son?"

"What about my ma? Where is she? I want to see her," Kenny said.

"I don't know where she is, son. I will do my best to find her."

"Will you bring her home when you do? She's all I got ... now Mary won't wake up."

"Come on, Kenny lad," Granny said, taking his hand in hers. "Let's get Jack some breakfast. He looks hungry."

Kenny wasn't hungry, his tummy felt funny, and he didn't know how the adults could talk about food, but maybe Jack was. He didn't think dogs would get the same feelings in their bellies. Would they?

CHAPTER 20

Kathleen looked up from her ledger when the door to the office opened. She was in the process of updating the cards the children would carry with them when they left on the next orphan train. Thanks to Bridget's and Carl's suggestions, each child now carried a card telling their new families their real names, last known address in New York, and the details of any siblings or other family members they might have. The hope was it would prevent children from getting lost in the system, like what had happened to Carl's sister Hope.

"Inspector Griffin is here to see Lily, Kathleen. I thought you might be able to help him. Shall I ask Cook to send up some tea?"

"That would be lovely. Thank you, Sheila." Kathleen smiled at the new maid before greeting the policeman. "Come in and warm yourself by the fire. That weather isn't getting any better, is it?"

"No, it isn't, Miss Collins."

Inspector Griffin almost took over the whole room being such a large, tall man. She guessed his imposing size came in handy for his job. He moved closer to the fire, holding out his hands to the heat. He wasn't wearing gloves, and his fingers looked red raw from the cold.

"Kathleen, Inspector Griffin. You always called me by my name."

"That was before you got all grown up. Imagine you running the sanctuary now. I didn't see that coming, I was sure you would head out to Wyoming like the rest of your family."

Kathleen closed over the ledger after marking where she had left off. She could finish the job later.

"I was, too, but when Lily fell pregnant again, someone had to step in. She's done so much for my family. It was the least I could do."

"Guess having a handsome, young doctor nearby would help, too, wouldn't it?"

Kathleen felt her cheeks go red as the inspector teased her over Richard. If she were honest, he was part of her reason for staying in New York. His studies to become a plastic surgeon kept him in the city.

"How are Bridget and Carl? I heard they were back in town," Inspector Griffin asked.

"They are. In fact, you just missed Bridget. She took some of the children down to see the window display in Macy's. It's a firm favorite."

"I like that window, too. From what I see, it isn't just for children. Or at least, that's my excuse," he said.

They were interrupted by Sheila returning with tea and a plate of freshly baked scones. "Cook said you were to take some home with you, Inspector. She has a small basket ready in the kitchen for when you leave."

"Please pass on my thanks. Cook knows how much I love her baking."

Sheila smiled self-consciously and let herself out of the room, closing the door behind her. Kathleen noted the bright expression fell from the Inspector's eyes before he turned to stare at the fire. She sensed something had upset him. In his line of work, he saw some dreadful things.

"How can we help you, Inspector? I guess this isn't a social call."

"No, Kathleen, it isn't, although I should have called to say hello before now. With the new reforms Roosevelt is pushing through, things have been rather busy."

"Richard told me all about that the last time we had dinner. It seems a number of your colleagues have found themselves on the wrong side of Mr. Roosevelt."

Inspector Griffin smiled. "That is an understatement, my dear. I have been saying for years that corruption is deep seated in the force. Up 'til now, nobody wanted to address it, but young Roosevelt knows what he is about. Wouldn't surprise me if he ended up as president one day."

"He seems like a good man," Kathleen replied. She glanced at her ledger and at once felt guilty for thinking about how busy she was. Lily had never made anyone feel uncomfortable or unwanted when they came to her for help. Kathleen decided she should mirror her friend and confidant.

"Kathleen, I know you are busy and have more than enough on your plate, but I need your help. I have to place a young boy."

"An orphan?"

"Well, the truth is, we don't know

whether he is or he isn't. His parents both ran away. Not together, mind you. The father deserted the family some time back, but now his mother has disappeared."

"Oh, the poor child. Doesn't he have any siblings?"

"Not anymore. The mother, well, she killed her daughter, Kenny's sister, before she left."

"Kenny? That name is familiar."

Inspector Griffith turned bright red, and it wasn't from the heat of the fire.

"Kathleen, forgive me. I forgot you once lived near the Flemings. Kenny Clark is the boy's name. His sister—"

"Mary Clark, she was about fourteen years old. Oh, my goodness, how could ... why would anyone .. .oh…"

"Yes, I know. It's horrible to think a mother could do that to her child, but unfortunately, it is not as uncommon as we would wish. We believe Mrs. Clark was rather intoxicated, not that the drinking excuses her behavior. From all accounts, she wasn't a pleasant woman, even when she was sober."

Kathleen could agree with that statement, but she wasn't about to judge the woman. Life was harsh in the tenements, and who knew what had happened to Mrs. Clark to drive her to drink.

"I only met her a few times. I met Mary and Kenny at Mrs. Fleming's. She used to feed them." Kathleen could remember her old friend with a smile now, although she would always miss her. She wasn't the only one, as Mrs. Fleming had helped countless people in the tenements and surrounding area.

"She was a saint, Mrs. Fleming. There's a number of children who miss her dreadfully, not just her own family," Inspector Griffin said.

Kathleen nodded her head in agreement. She missed Mrs. Fleming in a practical way, too, not just because of her kindness, but as someone who could help the sanctuary assist those in need. She was always able to point Lily toward the neediest families.

"Where is Kenny now, Inspector Griffin?"

"Staying with Granny Belbin. She is doing a wonderful job of looking after Jack and him, but she is an old lady. She doesn't have much money either, and young boys need clothes and eat a lot. They have hollow legs."

"Jack? She has taken in another orphan, too? Funny, I can't picture Granny Belbin taking children into her home. She came to live at the building shortly before we left to come here. She was always chasing the kids off and threatening to cast spells on them." Kathleen could see the dark-clad woman now, her black clothes covered with mud and other stains. She walked with a hump on her back, probably as a result of being bent over some work surface. She would have ended up stooped over, too, if she had continued working in the sweatshop that was Mr. Oak's factory.

"She's got a warm heart under that crusty, old exterior. Only I don't think she wants anyone to know it. Maybe she thinks people will take advantage. Anyway, can you help?"

"Of course we can. We don't have many children staying here at the moment. We sent another group off on the orphan train the week before Thanksgiving in the hope the season would open people's hearts and homes. Seems to have worked, too, given the reports we have had back," she said, taking up her cup of tea. She glanced at her visitor's face. He looked very tired and strained. "Would you like me to collect Kenny and Jack from Mrs. Belbin?"

"Would you Kathleen? I would bring them here, but I haven't seen my own bed for the last two days. I could fall asleep on my feet."

"Of course I can. Mini Mike or Tommy will come with me."

The look of tiredness disappeared suddenly, replaced by anger and concern. Inspector Griffin always protected his own, and he considered the sanctuary to be partly his project. Lily had told Kathleen a lot about the early days when this gentle giant of a man had helped, when the police had been less forthcoming than they could be.

"Are you still afraid of Oaks? I haven't heard of him giving you any trouble."

The policeman's concern made her feel guilty. She hadn't heard a word about her former employer's son. His threats to make her sister Bridget pay seemed to have amounted to nothing. "No, not at all. Tommy and Mini Mike always escort us when we visit the tenements. We haven't found out who robbed the sanctuary last year, well, I mean who helped Maura and her friends," Kathleen trailed off, embarrassed at bringing her sister's name into the conversation.

"I never would have thought a sister of Bridget's and yours would have robbed

Lily, but I guess you never know folk really. Have you heard anything from her?"

"No, nothing. Bridget won't have anything to do with her, but I would like to know she's safe. I guess you think I am too soft." She knew people thought she was, especially after going to find Shane and Michael. Poor Michael was still in prison and would likely stay there for the rest of his sentence. As for Shane, well the less said about him the better. She had hoped he would stay in Wyoming, but, although he had enjoyed seeing his siblings and meeting all their new friends at Bella's wedding, he hadn't liked the countryside. He'd insisted on returning to New York. She wasn't going to talk to Inspector Griffin of her fears that Shane had joined a gang. He may be a friend, but he was also the police.

"Not at all, Kathleen. It's hard to turn our back on family, even when they do things that upset us. I have made inquiries over the last year, but she seems to have disappeared into thin air."

"Bridget says Maura will turn up when she needs something, but I can't help thinking she needs our help." Kathleen was certain her sister had found herself in dire straits. Tommy and Mini Mike knew the man Maura had gotten involved with, and they didn't have anything good to say about him. Still, she had other things to worry about, such as Kenny.

"Should I go and collect him this evening, assuming Mike or Tommy is free to come with me?"

"As soon as you can would be my advice. We don't know if his mother will turn up again. Tell Tommy and Mini Mike I was asking for them. I never approach them on the street, as I would ruin their reputation." Inspector Griffin laughed at his own joke before taking his leave. "I best go down to cook and collect my basket. Don't want her in a temper with me. She scares me half to death."

CHAPTER 21

athleen laughed as the policeman headed off toward the kitchen. She couldn't imagine a man who dealt with the worst of New York society every day being scared of Cook.

Her good humor disappeared just as quickly as it had come. Mary Clark, dead at the hands of her mother. She said a quick prayer for the soul of the young girl before writing a note for Mini Mike. She would go collect Kenny as soon as one of the boys arrived to escort her. She went to the front door and whistled for a runner.

"Miss Kathleen. Want someone?" a young boy resembling a rather worn-out scarecrow came running, his smile lighting up his face. She recognized him immediately.

"Yes, please, Sammy. Could you find Mini Mike or Tommy? I need to go out and would appreciate their help."

"Sure thing, miss."

"Good boy. Here's a penny and a scone."

"Thanks, miss."

The boy took off, his bare feet leaving footprints in the snow. She wished she could find a way to convince Sammy to come and stay at the sanctuary, but he insisted on living on the street. He was waiting for his big brother or his da to find him. They had said they would come back, but given both had gone to sea, she didn't hold much hope. She could get him a pair of shoes, though. Surely, he wouldn't say no to having his feet covered.

* * *

"Why was Inspector Griffin here? Cook told me," Bridget said, as she walked into the office, bringing a cold draught of air with her.

"He needs me to go collect a little boy. Kenny Clark. You remember him?"

"Name rings a bell. Didn't he have a sister, too? We met them a few times in Mrs. Fleming's house."

"Yes, that's the same family. Seems Kenny's ma has gone missing."

"Oh, the poor children. Do you want me to come with you to collect him?"

"No, Bridget, you need to rest. You look tired after Macy's. But I didn't get to finish. Mary Clark is dead."

"Dead?"

"Yes, and it's even worse, because Inspector Griffin says her ma killed her."

Bridget sat down heavily on the sofa, her face a white mask. "What type of world do we live in? A mother killing her own child, but why? Mary was such a quiet girl from what I remember, although it's been a few years since I saw her."

"I have no idea. Maybe Kenny will know more. Anyway, he needs us, so I sent for Mini Mike and Tommy to come with me."

Bridget glanced at her.

"Don't look at me like that. I will be careful. The boys won't let anything happen to me."

"I know, but I can't help worrying. You're my little sister, even if you are practically running this place now," Bridget said. "It suits you. All this extra responsibility. It's like you were born to do this job."

Shocked at the praise, Kathleen didn't know what to say. She played with some paper on her desk to cover her embarrassment, and when she looked up at her sister, Bridget's eyes were closed. She immediately felt guilty. Her sister's heart wasn't strong, and maybe she had been overdoing it. She knew Bridget loved helping with the twins and with things at the sanctuary, but she had to make sure she took things easier. Kathleen pulled a blanket over her sister and went to find Sheila to tell her to let the girl sleep.

CHAPTER 22

*M*ini Mike arrived early in the evening, explaining Tommy was caught up in something and would meet them later, if they needed more help.

"It won't take long, Mike. Inspector Griffin asked me to collect two children from the tenements Mrs. Fleming lived in. They need shelter."

Mike chatted as they walked to her old home. She didn't want to waste money on a cab. She quite liked walking in the snow, liking the sound of the crunch under her new boots. She spoke to Mike about her wish to get Sammy a pair of new boots.

"I know where to pick up some good secondhand ones, Miss Kathleen. New ones will only get him into trouble. Kids out here will kill for a pair of boots."

Kathleen wasn't shocked, not anymore. There had been a time when such a thing would have upset her for days, but now she was a realist. Life on the streets was difficult, particularly for the children. No matter what they did to try to get out of their situation, someone came along to make sure they couldn't. New shoes were a red flag, and the last thing Sammy needed was more attention from the wrong people.

"Seems troubles have flared up again among the gangs?" she asked Mike who had his ear close to the ground.

"Monk Eastman is determined his crew will dominate, and he isn't afraid of anyone. Seems the police are just as afraid of him as the kids. There have been stories of some of his old friends going for a swim in the Hudson."

"A swim? In winter?"

"Miss Kathleen, it wasn't by choice. Most people don't tie cement rocks to themselves when going for a dip."

Kathleen shuddered. She had never met Monk Eastman, but she knew the man by reputation. If he was half as bad as the stories suggested, she never wanted to lay eyes on him.

As they neared the entrance to the tenements, some men called Mini Mike over. He was torn between going and escorting Kathleen.

"You go on and see what they want. They might have news. Follow me through when you can. You know I am safe now."

Reluctantly, he agreed, and she walked on ahead of him into the tenements. She found Granny Belbin's place easily, having remembered it from when she lived there. She knocked on the door and waited for the old woman to answer. Sometimes people just shouted at you to come in, but there was no reply to her knock. She was about to give up when she heard shuffling, and then the door opened. An old woman poked her head out, her face devoid of expression.

"Mrs. Belbin, my name is Kathleen Collins. I used to live upstairs next door to the Flemings. How are you?" Kathleen pretended not to notice the smell of the old woman. Her long nails were encrusted with dirt. She guessed it had been some years since the old lady had enjoyed a bath.

"What do you want? I ain't goin' nowhere with no do-gooder. I heard about how you put childer on them trains."

Taken aback by the woman's hostility, Kathleen tried again.

"Mrs. Belbin, I am not here to do anything but take care of Kenny and Jack. Inspector Griffin asked me to come to see you."

Kathleen hoped the mention of the kindly policeman would help, but it didn't.

"They ain't here. Goodbye." The old woman made to close her door, but Kathleen had not forgotten what she had learned from living in the tenements. She blocked the door with her shoe.

"Please let me help. Inspector Griffin told me what happened to Mary. She was a lovely, young girl. I would love to help her brother and his friend. Please."

The woman took another look at Kathleen, and her tone was less strident this time.

"I told ya, they is gone. They lit out of here the other night, and I ain't seen them since. Ungrateful little runt."

Kathleen saw the concern and fear in the woman's eyes, despite her belligerent stance. Before she could say anything, Mini Mike came up behind her.

"Granny, me old darling. You are looking fine, give us a big hug," Mini Mike said, before lifting the old woman off her feet.

"You put me down right now, you big

lump. Put me down, I said. Do I have to give you a thump?"

"Ah, Granny, don't be like that. It's me," Mike said. "Do you still keep toffee under your pillow? Like the old days?"

CHAPTER 23

Kathleen watched, bewildered as the old woman smiled up at Mini Mike, her face lighting up. "You are a sight for sore eyes, Michael Cullen. Why you ain't been round to see your granny?"

"I been busy, Granny. This here lady, Kathleen Collins, and her wonderful friend Lily Doherty, keep me running around. I go off in circles. So why are you standing on the doorstep? Why don't you put the kettle on, and I will pull up some chairs, just like we used to do? Come on, Kathleen, take the weight off."

Kathleen found herself pushed into a chair and Granny likewise. Thankful she had brought the gentle giant with her, she hid a smile at the way he handled Granny. All the bluster and defiance had gone, and in its place was a pleasant old lady. Kathleen couldn't tell exactly how old, but somehow, she guessed the woman wasn't as elderly as she first appeared.

"Granny, you look skinny. Nobody been feeding ya?"

"What did I teach you about making comments about a lady," Granny retorted sharply. "I don't need a lot, Michael. Now tell me how's Tommy? You keepin' him out of trouble like you promised?"

"Sure I am, Granny. We are regular altar boys now, the pair of us, aren't we, Kathleen?"

Kathleen decided not to venture an opinion. She didn't want Granny to throw them out.

"So, what's the story with the young

lads, Kenny and Jack? Kathleen was sent here to take them to the sanctuary."

"You can't. I keep telling ya. They ain't here. The pair of them took off."

"Why, Granny? Something spook them?" Mini Mike asked, looking the old woman straight in the eyes.

"Don't you take that tone with me, young man. I ain't too old I can't tan your backside just like the old days. I didn't do nuffink but feed that boy and his dog. But he wants his ma. Don't know why? The silly witch never gave him an ounce of love, but he says he needs her. Told me he was off to find her."

"Oh, the poor child. She could be any-where," Kathleen said.

"I knows that girl, but don't you think I didn't try to make him stay here. I couldn't keep an eye on him day and night, though. He must have snuck out when I was asleep. I thought he'd be back, but it's been two days and nights now and no sign of him. I got the young lads looking for him, but he just disappeared into thin air."

"Did you tell Inspector Griffin?"

"And set the coppers after a child? Risk sending Kenny into a jail? Get out of my house. Mini Mike, throw her out."

"Now, Granny, calm down. Kathleen only wants to help Kenny. She is a lovely lady. You should see how she looks after all those poor, little tykes that end up at the sanctuary."

"I heard all about her looking after them. Shipping those kids off to be slaves to Protestants and rich folk. Never thought I would see the day when an Irish woman would do that to her own people."

"Now, Granny, don't start getting all het up. That isn't what Miss Kathleen and Miss Lily do. That is what the gossips say they do, but I knows for a fact that ain't what it's like. They does their best to find good homes for those kids. They don't sacrifice them to nobody. You got stubborn in your old age. You never were this judgmental when you were younger. You told Tommy and me we had to see the good in people, not the bad. When did you stop taking your own advice?"

CHAPTER 24

To Kathleen's horror, the old woman didn't shout back at Mike but seemed to crumple in front of them. She started keening back and forth like someone at a wake. "I tried to help Mary, I did. I tried to tell her not to go, but she wouldn't listen. Nobody listens to me no more. I ain't useful," the old woman repeated over and over.

"Mike, stop it. You're upsetting her." Kathleen put her cup down, tea untasted, as she rushed to the older woman's side.

"Please, Mrs. Belbin, don't cry. Mike didn't mean to upset you."

"I tried to tell Mary to leave her ma be, but the girl just wouldn't listen. I knew her ma was a bad'un. She didn't have a nice bone in her body, that old witch, but even I never thought her capable of what she did."

"We know that, Mrs. Belbin. Nobody blames you for what happened to Mary. Mike didn't mean to upset you. He's just worried about Kenny and the other boy."

"What other boy?" The woman's rotting teeth and resulting bad breath brought a tear to Kathleen's eye.

"Jack. We were told he was with Kenny," Kathleen explained.

Granny started laughing, leaving Kathleen and Mike exchanging worried glances. Had the old lady lost her mind?

"Jack ain't a kid. He's a half-starved mongrel Kenny found on a street corner and insisted on bringing home. I've been feeding it and keeping it here, as Kenny's ma would have killed him for it."

As if realizing what she just said, Granny fell silent. Kathleen patted her hand not knowing what to say to comfort her.

"Granny, be nice to Kathleen. She helps the children just like you do, only she don't hide her nice side. She's my friend, and you always said my friends were welcome at your fireside."

Granny gave Mike a glance and then turned her attention to Kathleen.

"Go on, Granny. Say yer sorry, and then we can all be friends. Else I'm off." Mini Mike stood up. Granny sighed, as if acknowledging she was beaten.

"I'm sorry for being off with ya. I just don't take kindly to strangers." At Mike's cough, Granny continued. "But any friend of Mike is welcome. Would you like a bit of milk for your tea? I got some somewhere."

The thought of drinking the tea which was swimming in grease and goodness knew what else, given the dirt of the cups, turned Kathleen's stomach.

"No, thank you, Mrs. Belbin. I just finished a cup before we came out to visit."

"Call me Granny, dear. Now tell me what I can do to help you find Kenny."

Kathleen asked for a description of Kenny, in particular what he was wearing, and when Granny had last seen him. "Did he say anything giving you a hint where he might be going?"

"He said he knew someone who could find his ma. He wouldn't tell me who. I have no idea who he meant. I thought it might be the policeman, but now you are here, I can forget that idea. A priest maybe? But he didn't like the local priest..."

"Father Nelson?" Kathleen mused. "He's a lovely man, and the children usually love him. Wonder why Kenny didn't like him?"

"No, not him. The other fella. Draper or whatever his name is. I don't go to church, not anymore."

"Granny don't go, ever since the priest told her to leave," Mini Mike explained. "He said havin' a baby without a man was a sin.

Granny should have belted him. I would have."

"Michael Cullen, you would not," Granny scolded. "Did I not teach you better? Nothing to be gained by using your fists."

Fascinated by the interaction between the two people and also learning about Mini Mike's upbringing kept Kathleen silent. She could imagine a priest doing exactly what Mike had described. Before Father Nelson had arrived, they had another priest who used to call out unmarried mothers. She didn't see where it said in the Bible you had to love everyone but those who had children out of wedlock. Didn't make sense to her. But she wasn't about to get into a discussion about religion. She had a child to find in the middle of a very cold winter.

"Granny, we will be off now. I need to find Kenny. Please let us know by sending a lad over to the sanctuary, if he comes back here."

Kathleen handed the old woman a penny.

"What's this for? I don't take charity."

"It's not for you, Granny. It's for the boy you send with a message," Kathleen replied hastily, not wanting to injure the old woman's pride, although it was obvious from the fact she was skin and bones, she could have done with the money. She resolved to get Cook to make up one of her special baskets and have Mike deliver it. Or Tommy, whom she guessed would be pleased to see his Granny, too.

CHAPTER 25

"Is Granny Belbin your real granny?" Kathleen asked, as they walked back to the sanctuary.

"No, Miss Kathleen. I never knew my parents, or my grandparents. I grew up a bit away from here, closer to the center of Five Points. Tommy and me was with some other kids. Granny lived there, too. She used to feed us and look after us. She used to make us have baths. You can't imagine it now, but she used to chase us around the courtyard with her broom, until we washed our ears and necks. She was a wonderful woman, but, oh man, her temper was awful. We was more afraid of her than anyone else. Guess that's why me and Tommy didn't get in trouble with the law. Granny would have killed us if we landed in jail. I never knew she had moved here. Feel bad I haven't been checkin' in on her."

"You were lucky she cared so much about ye. What about her child?"

"She ain't never had children, least not that I know of," Mike said.

"But I thought you said the priest threw her out of the church?" Kathleen asked.

"Aye, he did, but she never had the baby. It died. But that wasn't why that priest hated her. See, she protected us from everyone, even those who were supposed to be looking after us, if you know what I mean."

Kathleen wasn't exactly sure she understood, but, sensing he was embarrassed, she changed the subject.

"Mike, how are we going to find Kenny? Granny said she had sent the boys from the tenements out looking. If they couldn't find him, how will we?"

"I don't rightly know, Miss Kathleen. That's something we got to pray about. God will send his answer. We just need to make sure we hear it."

Stunned by his devotion, Kathleen fell silent. Of course, she believed in God and would pray for his help, but she couldn't sit waiting at the sanctuary, when a child was in need. She would speak to Lily and Charlie, in case they had more ideas. Richard would help her too. He dealt with many children at the hospital, so he might know of more places where Kenny might be hiding out. She would also speak to Inspector Griffin. If the police knew the places Kenny's ma might have frequented, maybe they could find the boy there.

CHAPTER 26

*K*enny dragged himself through the snow. He couldn't feel his feet—they were frozen solid. Jack kept running back and forth, almost tripping him up at times, so he'd picked up the puppy and put him inside his jacket. The dog must have been cold, as he promptly fell asleep in the warmth, his breath keeping Kenny's chest warm.

He wasn't sure whether he was going in the right direction. He had to find Santa Claus, so he could give Kenny his family back for Christmas. Mary had said Santa

Claus was magical, and he had to make a wish. This was such an important wish. He thought he better go and meet the man in person. Mary had taken him to see the window display at Macy's last week. It had been magical with scenes from various books, including his favorite, *Gulliver's Travels*. Not that he could read that book, but Mary had read it to him. Their Dad had left a copy of it behind when he left. Mary said that meant Dad had gone away to sea, just like Gulliver, and was traveling to meet different people and see other worlds. Kenny wished his dad had taken them all with him. Then maybe Ma wouldn't be so sad and horrid all the time. And Mary. He swallowed hard, not wanting to think about his sister. They had been lying to him when they told him she was dead. She couldn't be. She'd promised to always look after him.

"Hey, you. What you doin'?"

"Nuffink," Kenny whispered, his voice not working properly, as he stared at the boys blocking his way. They looked mean, and he didn't think he would be able to fight them. They were bigger than he was.

"You can't be doing nuffink. You is up to somefink. I can tell. What you got there?" The boy indicated the mound, where Jack was under his jacket.

"It's nuffink, I told ya," Kenny spoke louder this time.

"Get him, boys. I bet he's got something to eat under there."

All at once, a group of boys jumped on him. He didn't stand a chance. They ripped his coat away, and Jack tumbled to the ground. He made a grab for the puppy, but the group prevented him from reaching Jack.

Jack barked loudly, but, when a boy hit Kenny, the puppy growled and bared his teeth. The guilty boy took a step back, but the leader of the group aimed a kick at Jack. Kenny dived to protect his dog and got kicked painfully in the ribs.

"That's enough. Stop it, all of you," a youngster shouted. She sounded like a girl, but she was dressed in boys' clothes. She came and stood over Kenny. "Any of ye lay another finger on him, you got me to deal with it. You hear?"

"What you goin' to do to us?" one of the boys said, sneering at her.

"Me? Nothing. But my brothers will knock ten bells out of each of you. You know that."

CHAPTER 27

Kenny had no idea who his savior was, but the boys who had picked on him melted away. She stood, hands on hips, until the very last one had left. Then she reached down and helped him to his feet. She put her hand on Jack, too. Kenny couldn't believe it when the dog didn't growl but licked her fingers.

"He's cute," she said. "What do you call him?"

"Jack."

"Stupid name for a dog."

"Is not. It suits him. Anyways, he's my

dog, and I'll call him what I like." Kenny couldn't stop the dart of jealousy filling him as Jack licked the stranger like she was his best friend.

"Suit yourself," the girl said, shrugging. "Where are you off to? Home?"

Kenny was going to lie, but something stopped him. "I got to get to Macy's," he blurted out.

"Macy's Department Store? What does someone like you want down there?"

"I got to see a man. That's all." Kenny felt stupid now as she stared at him.

"When did you last eat?" she asked.

"What?" Kenny asked, not following the change in subject.

"You simple or something? I asked you when you last had something to eat? Jack looks hungry."

"He's always starving," Kenny agreed.

"Come on then. I got to get dinner on for my brothers. You can have some, too, if you help me carry this lot home."

Kenny looked at her bags and nodded.

He knew he shouldn't go with strangers, but he was starving, and she had saved him from those boys. Her hat fell off, as she bent to get the bags, allowing her long dark hair to fall freely on her shoulders. She impatiently gathered it in a messy bun before putting her hat back on.

"How old are you? You seem a bit young to be out here alone, even with the dog."

"I'm old enough," Kenny said. "I'll be six soon."

"Ah, that's young."

"You don't look that old either."

"Cheeky," the girl replied. "I'm fifteen, sixteen on Christmas day."

Kenny didn't reply, his gaze fixed on the potatoes in the bag.

"Ain't you ever seen a potato?" the girl asked him.

"Yeah, of course. I just … where do you live then?"

"Over there behind those factories. Not too far. Where're your shoes? Did those boys nick them?"

"Not those boys," Kenny said. "I got in trouble before."

"What do they call you then, mouse?"

"Kenny."

"I'll call you Mouse. You look like one."

Kenny didn't like that idea at all, but she had food and shelter, and he needed both. So, if he had to put up with a stupid name for a few hours, so be it.

"Why did those boys run when you mentioned your brothers?" he asked, curiosity getting the better of him.

"Cause they know I am right. Anyone put a hand on me, and the lads will skin them alive. Everyone knows my brothers. They run with the Eastmans. You heard of them?"

Kenny shook his head.

"Who hasn't heard of the Eastmans? Don't matter. You'll get to meet them tonight. Right, let's go. Come on, Jack. I got a bone for you."

Jack, traitor that he was, set off walking after the girl with his tail wagging high behind him. The girl stopped to look behind at him. "Are you coming or not?"

Kenny shrugged his shoulders. He might as well. It wasn't as if he had a better offer.

"What's your name?"

"Anichka but my friends call me Angel."

"Can you slow down a little, Angel. I'm tired."

She turned and waited until he caught up with her, and together they made their way to her home, a small apartment above a shop. It was much grander than where he lived. He cleaned his feet on the mat, belatedly remembering his manners. Mary would be proud of him. He shook his head, not wanting to think of his sister. He would cry, and then Angel would think he was a baby.

ANGEL WAS A GOOD COOK, better than Mary, if the food tasted as good as it smelled. She had given him some bread and butter to eat while they waited for her brothers. He wondered if they would let him stay. The other boys had been frightened of them. What if they didn't like him and kicked him out. Or worse?

As he ate the bread, he looked around the kitchen, which boasted a large table and chairs, some wooden presses, and a big stove. They didn't cook on the open fire as Mary had. The rooms were situated over a store, not other rooms like the ones he lived in. He didn't know how many rooms the family had, as Angel had gone upstairs to get something. It was quieter than he was used to and not just because her brothers weren't home. There wasn't the same noise from other families. Even the street outside seemed quieter. It was clean and tidy. He guessed Angel was like Mary, who liked things to be kept straight. There were no holy pictures around. He was used to seeing pictures of Jesus and Mary. He wondered if they kept them upstairs.

CHAPTER 28

A thud and a shout alerted Kenny someone was coming. He shrank back into the wall, his hand on Jack's neck.

"That will be my brothers. You can stop looking so scared. They won't eat you. They are nice to their friends."

Kenny didn't reply but kept his eyes on the door. It opened, and three giants walked in, each one taller than the one before. They had to stoop down to come through the door.

"What you got here, Angel?" one of them asked.

"Mouse and Jack," she replied.

"I take it the boy is Mouse?" one of the men said, his eyes teasing.

"Me name is Kenny, and this is me dog, Jack."

"Nice to meet you, Kenny. I'm Lucky, this here is Axel, and that big lump over there is Haviv."

Kenny nodded, his sudden bravery having disappeared at the sight of the scar on Axel's face.

"What you doing on this side of town? You're Irish, ain't ya?" Lucky asked. "You a five-pointer?"

"Yes, sir. I'm Irish. I don't know about a five-pointer."

"I like you already, kid. He called me sir."

"Sit down and eat. I'm starving," Axel ordered. Kenny assumed he was the oldest, given how he took charge.

He sat next to Angel, who served up a large dish of meatballs and something stringy. He had never seen anything like it before. He wasn't sure how to eat it.

"You lost your appetite?" Angel challenged him.

"No. I was just waitin'."

"So how did you find Kenny?" Axel asked his sister.

"A group of boys was picking on Jack and him, so I told them you would see them off. He was hungry, and I took him home. He needs to get to Macy's."

"What you want with the store? They got lots of security working. You'll get caught if you plan on robbing it," Lucky said in between large mouthfuls.

"I'm no thief," Kenny retorted quickly. "I got to see a man is all."

"What type of man?" Axel asked.

Kenny didn't want to admit he was going to see Santa. He figured they would laugh at him.

"I asked you a question."

At the threatening look Axel sent his way, Kenny lost all his bravado.

"I got to meet Santa Claus. I want him to

give me back me ma and me sister. The police said Mary was dead, but I knows he's lying, and she was just asleep. Mary said Santa was magic, that he can do stuff. I want me ma back, too."

CHAPTER 29

*H*e couldn't help the tears falling, despite wanting to look like a grown up in front of Angel. He rubbed his arm across his nose, as Jack inched closer to him. He wanted to run away.

"Listen, kid, why don't you eat your dinner, and then you can tell us your story." Axel gestured at his plate.

Kenny nodded, not sure how much he could eat with the lump in his throat. He glanced at Angel, but she wasn't laughing at him. She gave him a smile and picked up her fork. He watched as she wrapped the white strings around her fork. He tried to do the same, but it kept falling off.

"What's wrong with you? You never eat spaghetti before?"

"No," Kenny admitted. "But it's delicious."

"Here, kid, like this," Lucky showed him how to manage the meal. He wasn't entirely successful, but at least he got almost as much in his mouth as he did on his chin. It was the best thing he had ever tasted. The meatballs were rich and spicy, not bland like the food he was used to.

"Did you get anything for afters, Angel?" Lucky asked.

"I didn't have time to bake, but I picked up some pastries. I was keeping them for Sunday, but you can have them now, if you want."

"You are an angel. Lucky, put some coffee on," Axel ordered, as he lit up a cigarette.

"You put the coffee on. I ain't your wife,"

Lucky retorted, but, before he had barely finished the sentence, Axel sprang out of the chair and pushed his brother up against the wall, Lucky's hand twisted painfully behind his back.

"Let go, you big lump. I'll do it," Lucky shouted.

Kenny glanced at Angel, but she didn't seem to notice the violence going on around her. She sat finishing the remains of her dinner.

"Angel's been working hard all day making us this food. You guys show some respect," Haviv said, putting the kettle on the fire to boil. He added some coffee to a pot and then poured the hot water on top. A beautiful aroma filled the room. Kenny had never tasted coffee before. He hoped the brothers would let him try it, although he felt rather sleepy after the meal.

"You okay there, kid? You look like you'll fall asleep in your plate any second."

Kenny sat straighter in response to Axel's remark.

Haviv poured coffee for all of them, including Kenny. He added some sugar before handing the cup to the boy. Kenny tasted the drink. Yuck. It had smelled so good, but he preferred tea. He wasn't about to say that, though.

"Kid, tell us again why you want to go to Macy's. What's this about your sister and your ma?" Axel asked, lighting a second cigarette from the butt of the first.

Kenny told him his story. He didn't cry this time, but he stumbled over some of the words. It was hard talking about Mary. He missed her more than his ma.

"Jeez, you had it tough, kid. You got somewhere to stay tonight?" Axel asked, setting his cup down on the table.

Kenny shook his head.

"You can stay here with us," Axel offered. "We got plenty of room. Tomorrow afternoon, we'll take you down to Macy's, and you can see Santa and ask him whatever you like."

"Don't go making promises to the boy,"

Lucky warned. "Seeing Santa costs money."

"I know that," Axel said. "I'll pay for him. Can't have a kid miss out at Christmas, now can we?"

Kenny didn't hear the rest of the conversation, having lost his battle. His head would have landed in the plate of food but for Angel's quick response.

"Sounds like he had a lucky escape with a ma like his," Lucky said.

"It's sad and all that, but he ain't our problem," Axel shot back. "We got bigger fish to fry. We have to get out of New York. Let the heat simmer down a little. Eastman is out for blood."

"Shoot, it wasn't our fault the guard got killed. We didn't know Monk had that place under his personal protection," Haviv protested.

"Don't matter. We are going in the river if we don't get clear," Axel responded grimly.

"Where do you suggest we go?"

"I don't know. What about Uncle Asael's

place out in Maine? Quiet enough down there. Aunt Rachel keeps writing, telling us to come and meet some nice Jewish girls. Maybe Santa can give you a bride for Christmas." Lucky's remark earned him a belt across the ear from Axel.

"Ah, man, she keeps kosher. She'd have us committed herself for not observing Shabbat," Haviv moaned.

"She might have us praying, but at least we'd be alive. More than can be said if we stay around Monk!" Axel stood up as he spoke.

"What will we do with the kid?" Haviv asked.

"Take him with us? He got nothing left in New York. Maybe Aunt Rachel can find him a wife?" Axel replied, picking Kenny up with a surprisingly gentle touch. Kenny opened his eyes and smiled up at the man who had promised to pay for him to see Santa. Then he closed them again and fell back into a deep sleep, totally unaware of the plans being made for his future.

CHAPTER 30

*K*enny woke to Jack licking his face and pulling at his ear.

"What's up with ya? Ya daft, mutt," he said affectionately, as he cradled the dog to him. The rest of the room was in silence but for the snores of Angel's older brothers echoing through the upstairs floorboards. He got up quietly, so as not to wake them. Moving to the door of the room, he spotted Angel in the kitchen area poking the fire.

She glanced at him as he came in but didn't say anything. He thought she looked as if she had been crying. Girls did that a lot.

"Um, Jack needs to go out."

"Let him out that door," she said, pointing. "Keep an eye, though, that he won't run away. I'm not running after him."

Confused by her crankiness, he did as she said. Jack was soon finished and back indoors.

"Close that door. You're letting all the heat out."

Kenny blew through his nose. It was a game he had once played with Mary, pretending he was an animal with the steam coming out his nostrils, but Angel didn't look amused. If anything, she looked sadder.

"What's the matter with you? Don't you want to leave?" he asked, keeping his distance in case his questions earned him a belt.

"No, I don't. I hate our aunt. She'll make me wear dresses and study. She'll even force me to go to school and take up needlework," Angel said.

"So why do you have to go then? Can't you tell your brothers you want to stay here?"

"I can, but they won't listen. You heard them last night."

"I don't know who they were talking about," Kenny said.

"You never heard of Monk Eastman? Where've you been living? He runs New York."

"I thought that was some fella called Roosevelt. Inspector Griffin mentioned him a few times." Kenny didn't know or care who ran New York. All he cared about was the fact he was hungry. He wondered if Angel was going to feed him again.

"Kenny, you should go now, before the boys wake up. I should never have brought you here," Angel said, almost pushing him out the door.

"No, I don't want to. Lucky said he

would take me to see Santa, and he can give me my family back. Why are you being so mean?"

"Yes, Angel. Why are you throwing our young friend out?"

Kenny saw the look of fear on Angel's face before she turned her attention back to the fire. Lucky glanced his way, a smile on his face, but Kenny didn't feel as comfortable as he had the night before. Jack growled but stayed close to Kenny, making him wonder what the dog had against this giant of a man.

"Sit yourself down, kid. We goin' to have some breakfast, and then you'll have a bath. Afterward, we will get ourselves up to Macy's. You can see Santa, and I got a job to do. We will be back here in time for dinner. You'll see."

Kenny was about to protest the bath, but Angel got in before him.

"What type of job, Lucky? He ain't nothin' more than an innocent kid."

"I bet when you give him a wash, he will clean up real nice. That hair and those baby blues will have the ladies swooning over him."

Ladies? What was Lucky talking about? Kenny was only interested in seeing Santa.

"Lucky, don't we have enough trouble?" Angel asked.

"Angel, you stick to doing what you do best and leave the thinking to me. Do you have anything Kenny can wear? Those clothes he has are little better than rags."

Kenny pulled his sweater closer. Sure, it was ripped and torn, but Mary had knit it for him. He scratched his hair as he watched Lucky warily keeping his distance, but the man didn't say another word. He sat at the table and shoveled big mouthfuls of oatmeal into him.

"Sit down and eat. If you wait 'til Axel gets up, there will be nothing left," Lucky said as he beckoned Kenny to the table.

Kenny sat, but his appetite had disappeared. He didn't like the way things were turning. He didn't want a bath or a change of clothes, and he wasn't at all sure going to see Santa with Lucky was a good idea. Still, what was his alternative? He didn't reckon he would get far if Lucky were to chase after him.

CHAPTER 31

"Mornin'. What's got you in such a good mood?" Axel asked, as he entered the room, his scar looking more vivid in his freshly washed face.

"Got a way out of our troubles, Axel. Thought of it last night. Monk is going to be so pleased with us. We won't have to go near Aunt Rachel."

Axel glanced at Angel, but Kenny saw she didn't look up from the fire. He looked down before the man could catch his eye.

"You going to tell me your plan, Lucky?"

"Later," Lucky said. Angel, that water ready yet? Where's your scissors, reckon the kid needs a haircut, too."

Kenny stood up quickly. "I don't need nothing. I got to get home. I forgot, but I promised Granny Belbin I'd clean her windows today. Thank you so much for having me."

Kenny didn't get far, as Lucky's arm stretched out to grab his wrist in a tight grip.

"Now that's not how it works, Kenny lad. We fed you, and you are going to do us a little favor in return. I scratch your back, and you scratch mine. That's the way it is in these parts."

Kenny knew when he was beaten and sat back down. Axel stood to help Angel take down the tin bath and place it in front of the fire. Angel filled it with steaming water, testing it with her elbow to make sure it wasn't too hot.

"In you go," Lucky ordered.

"In front of all of ye?" Kenny protested,

but his answer was to land in the bath fully clothed. Angel squealed, as the water splashed her, the fire sizzled, and Axel threw something at Lucky for making him wet. Lucky just laughed, but it wasn't a sound Kenny wanted to hear again. He looked for Jack, but the puppy had taken refuge under a chair on the opposite side of the room from Lucky.

"Best do as he says," Angel whispered, handing Kenny a flannel and a small piece of soap. "I'll wash your hair for you."

As she did, the tears ran down Kenny's face, but he had his back to the boys, so they couldn't see him. Angel's gentle touch reminded him of Mary. He wished his sister were there, but then he doubted he would be sitting in this house. Mary would never have accepted Angel's invitation to eat something.

Soon he didn't recognize himself. Angel had found some old clothes—a pair of trousers and a shirt with a jacket that was only slightly too big for him. His hair was sitting against his neck, rather than curling on his collar, following the haircut Lucky had administered. He gazed at his feet, hoping Lucky would be pleased with his new look.

"Don't he look as innocent as a newborn babe?" Lucky asked Axel and Haviv.

"Not sure your plan is going to work, Lucky," Axel said, looking at Kenny doubtfully.

"It will. It has to," Lucky retorted sharply. "Right, young man, let's get going."

Jack moved toward Kenny's feet, but Lucky aimed a kick at the dog. Thankfully, Jack was too quick for him and sprang out of the way.

"What you do that for?" Kenny cried. "You could have killed him."

Lucky grabbed Kenny's arm, squeezing it painfully. "Leave the dog with Angel. You can't take it into Macy's anyway."

"But he comes with me everywhere," Kenny protested, not liking the way his voice shook.

"He stays here. Now come on, or Santa will have gone back to the North Pole at this rate." Lucky laughed at his joke, but nobody else joined in. Kenny kissed Jack goodbye quickly and then turned to follow Lucky. "Look after Jack for me please, Angel," he whispered.

She didn't look up as he left, but he prayed she had heard him. Lucky walked so fast he had to run to keep up with the tall man.

CHAPTER 32

*B*ack at the sanctuary, the children and adults had gathered in the sitting room.

"Shush, children, keep your eyes closed. No peeking," Kathleen admonished the children, as they giggled and shut their eyes. Bridget held Teddy in her arms, with Carl holding Laurie. Both twins were angels, a good thing considering Lily was due to have her next baby just after Christmas.

"Can we open them yet, Miss Kathleen?"

"No George, not yet, just keep your eyes closed for a couple seconds more. Okay, let's count down—three, two, and one. You can open them now."

Kathleen stood back as the children opened their eyes and stared at the huge Christmas tree sitting pride of place in what was usually the sewing room. Richard stood beside it, his grin almost as big as the children's.

"So, who is going to be the first to decorate the tree?" Richard asked, looking at Kathleen.

"George won the chance to go first. Go on, George, put your decoration on."

"I don't know where would be best?" George said, sticking his tongue out, as he stared at the tree.

"Want me to pick you up, so you can reach up high?" Richard asked him. George nodded as he took the string of popcorn Kathleen had helped him with and started winding it around the upper branches of the tree.

"Can we all put our decorations on now, Miss Kathleen?"

"Certainly, Carrie. Off you go, and don't get in each other's way."

The children ran toward the tree, but thankfully, they helped rather than hindered each other's progress.

"Miss Kathleen, would you like a cup of my mulled wine? I made it myself from a family recipe," Cook offered.

"Yes, thank you. I am sure the gentlemen would enjoy a glass, too."

"They are on seconds already," Cook confided in a whisper. "Don't judge Doc Richard harshly. He came in chilled to the bone. It will help warm the cockles of his heart."

Kathleen exchanged a grin with Lily. They had discussed the fact Cook never seemed as concerned about their chilled bones as she did for Richard, Charlie, or Carl, or Father Nelson for that matter. Cook treated every man, regardless of his age, occupation, or status, as if he were her own long-lost son.

"What are your plans for tomorrow, Kathleen?" Lily settled herself on the chair.

"I thought I would take the children to see the Macy's window. Bridget says it is stunning this year. She said the window dressers outdid themselves. Would you like to come?" Kathleen offered, as she took Teddy from Bridget. She loved holding Lily's babies. "Bridget won't be joining us, as Richard says she needs a day off."

"I am fine, and Richard is just being a fusspot," Bridget protested, earning herself a reprimanding look from her husband as well as her doctor.

"I would love to, but I don't think I would fit. This baby seems heavier than the last time around," Lily said, caressing her bump.

"Maybe it's another set of twins."

"Kathleen Mary Collins," Lily gasped. "Don't you wish that on me. I love the boys, but one extra baby is enough for me. I don't know how I would manage without Vicky to help me. She is a godsend."

Kathleen didn't disagree. Vicky had been another one of Mrs. Fleming's protégés. When their old neighbor died, Vicky came to live at the sanctuary. She loved little children and had jumped at the chance to help Lily with looking after the boys. Vicky regularly came into the sanctuary to help look after any children who needed shelter. She was a firm favorite amongst the children, possibly because she behaved like a child herself. As Kathleen glanced toward the tree, she saw Vicky had climbed the ladder and was swaying precariously trying to add decorations to the top.

"Vicky thinks she is a cat with nine lives," Lily said, as she followed Kathleen's gaze. "Lucky Richard is on hand to deal with any emergencies should she fall." Lily took a drink of tea, having complained the smell of mulled wine turned her stomach.

CHAPTER 33

*K*enny struggled to keep up with Lucky until they arrived at 18th Street and Broadway.

"Keep close to me, kid. I do the talkin', and you just look dumb and sad."

"But I need to speak to Santa," Kenny protested.

"You want to see your dog again, don't ya?" Lucky hissed at him.

Kenny nodded mutely.

"You got a baby face, and these ladies are going to love ya. I need money, and you are my golden ticket. Now start crying."

"But I..." Kenny didn't get to finish his sentence, as Lucky twisted his fingers painfully, bringing real tears to his eyes. The tall boy grinned, as the tears flowed down Kenny's face.

"Now go over and tell that lady over there you are lost. Go on. Tell her you was with me, your older brother, and you can't find me."

Kenny wanted to say no, but he was too scared. Not of what would happen to him but to Jack. He wished he had never met Angel.

He walked slowly in the direction of the woman, rubbing his face in his sleeve. He glanced behind him to see Lucky staring at him with a menacing look on his face. Kenny stumbled, almost falling into the woman.

"Sorry missus, I didn't see ya," he mumbled.

"Oh, would you look at him, Cecilia. Isn't he the sweetest child you ever saw? Look at those curls. Where are your parents, child?"

Kenny shrugged his shoulders.

"Are you lost?" the woman asked him, looking concerned.

Kenny nodded, following Lucky's instructions. The woman called a member of staff over who looked at Kenny suspiciously.

"Yes, Mrs. Armstrong?"

"Donald, this young man is lost. Can you find his parents?"

"Our store is quite large. It could take some time," the man said, now glaring at Kenny. The tears came easier this time. He sensed he was in trouble, but he wasn't sure how to fix things.

"Child, what do your parents look like?"

"My brother brought me to see Santa. I have to see Santa." Kenny wasn't acting now. He was desperate to see the magical man who would give him back his family.

"Oh, you poor child. Let's take him to see Santa, and maybe his brother will be looking for him there. If not, we can call the police. I am sure they will be able to find his parents and home."

"It would be best to call the police now, ma'am," the clerk replied.

"Nonsense. Let him speak to Santa first. My own children used to love doing that," the lady replied firmly. "Come along child. What do they call you?"

"Kenny. I mean Kenneth, ma'am."

"Come along, Kenneth. Let's go find Santa Claus."

Kenny looked around but couldn't see Lucky. He followed the woman, his enthusiasm to see Santa tempered by the knowledge the police would be called. Would he be locked up? If he was, he wouldn't be able to find his ma or Mary.

He trailed after the woman, his reluctance to meet the magic man growing. What if Santa knew Lucky was up to no good? Kenny knew Lucky was doing something bad, but he wasn't sure what it was. Santa would know, too, and Kenny would get the blame.

"There you are, dear. That's the queue for Santa. Do you have your list of what you want? My sons always had a list a mile long."

The woman kept talking, and Kenny lost track of what she was saying. He found it difficult to concentrate as the heat of the shop and his fear of being taken away by the police increased.

"What will you ask for?" the woman asked, her tone suggesting it wasn't for the first time.

"I want him to find my ma and Mary," he blurted out. "They went and left me."

"I thought it was your brother who left you, Kenneth," the woman said.

"He did, but my ma and Mary left me before that. I want Santa to find them. Will he do that?" Kenny asked the woman, staring up at her face to make sure he heard her answer.

"I am sure he will help, but why don't you ask him for a toy as well. He has to put a toy in his sack for you when he visits on Christmas Eve."

"I don't want anything else. Just Mary," Kenny repeated, knowing the woman would think he was ungrateful, but it was true. Before Mary had been hurt, he had wanted a red fire engine. He had seen it in the window of Macy's when his sister brought him down to see the window display. The little wooden engine was painted bright red and took pride of place in one of the windows. Mary had explained they couldn't afford it, but he had told her he was going to ask Santa for it. Now he couldn't care less about that engine. He wanted his sister.

"There you are, Kenneth. You are up next," the woman said, as she pushed him forward.

CHAPTER 34

Kenny approached the smiling Santa cautiously, his heart thudding against his chest. Santa was an old man, judging by his eyes and the length of his beard. He had a big fat stomach, too. He smiled at Kenny, but the smile faltered slightly, as Kenny didn't smile back. His face was frozen with fear.

"So, tell me young man, have you been a good boy?"

Kenny didn't respond, feeling Santa knew everything about him. Was it his fault his ma had run off after hurting Mary? Maybe she'd found out about Jack.

"What is your name?" Santa asked gently.

"Kenny, I mean Kenneth," he answered. "I need you to find my ma and my sister. Can you do that? Mary said you were magic."

Santa looked from him to Mrs. Armstrong and back.

"Isn't that your mother?"

"No, sir. Ma ran off, and I need you to bring her back, so I can go home. I want to go home." The tears fell in earnest now with Santa staring at him. Santa stood up, and before Kenny knew what was happening, he was sitting on the big man's knee.

"Kenny, tell me your story," Santa whispered.

Kenny gulped a couple of times to stop the tears. Then he whispered his story to Santa, starting with how his wonderful sister told him Santa was magical. The big man didn't say a word but listened to Kenny, as if he had all the time in the world. The queue of children increased, but when a manager came forward to have words with him, Mrs. Armstrong sent him off with his tail between his legs. Kenny smiled at the lady who winked at him before turning back to Santa and telling him everything, including how he happened to be here on his lap.

"Listen to me now, Kenny. You can't be walking the streets with just anyone. Does this man Lucky scare you?"

Kenny darted a quick look over his shoulder, but he couldn't see Lucky anywhere. He nodded.

"I have an idea. Why don't you stay here with me, as one of my helpers, and then, when the store closes, I will take you to a friend of mine. She runs a house for children. She will look after you and help you find your ma. Would that be okay?"

"You can do it? You can find my ma?

Can you get Jack back, too? I don't mean to be greedy, but Jack is just a puppy and needs me to look after him. Lucky has him."

"I will try," the older man with the white beard promised.

"You're the best. Thank you, Santa," Kenny said, wrapping his arms around the old man's neck.

"Good boy. Now I must see what the next child wants for Christmas, but if you ask Mrs. Armstrong to come closer, I will explain to her what we have agreed."

Kenny jumped down and went over to Mrs. Armstrong, telling the lady that Santa had asked for him to be his helper. Mrs. Armstrong questioned Santa and seemed satisfied with his answers. She took a card from her bag and handed it to Kenny. "You are a lovely young man. If you ever need me, come to this address. I hope you find your family. Happy Christmas, Kenneth."

"Merry Christmas to you, too, Mrs. Armstrong," he replied, as he took up his place at Santa's right hand. His job was to chat with the next child waiting to see Santa. As Mary often told him, he could talk to a wall, so the next couple of hours passed quickly.

CHAPTER 35

Kathleen waited in line at Macy's, the group of children with her all shouting and laughing as their excitement bubbled over. She was thrilled by their reactions, while at the same time wondering if bringing them there was the correct thing to do. People who donated to the sanctuary might not approve of her taking children on a frivolous trip. But it was Christmastime, and these kids had little to nothing. Soon they would be leaving New York in a search for their happy ever after. Many would find it, but some wouldn't. She had accepted that was part of the risk of trying to find these children new homes. The reality was that leaving them on the streets of New York would certainly result in abuse and death. At least by taking them on the trains, they had better odds of finding a family to provide them with food and shelter and, if they were lucky, love.

"Penny for them?" Richard asked her, as he came back from taking two of the boys to the restroom.

"I was just wondering what our sponsors would say to this trip. We could have used this money for a lot of other things."

"And miss this?" he asked. "Look at their little faces. Christmas is a time of magic. Stop worrying and start smiling. Go on. Let the Christmas spirit take over your heart, too."

She would, if there were room in her heart for anything but him. She looked away quickly for fear he would see her feelings.

"Miss Kathleen, will Santa give us new families?" George asked, looking up at her.

"Not today, but you can ask him to pray you find a lovely home in the spring. My sister Bridget and her husband Carl will take you and the rest of your friends to your new homes on their next trip."

"Will you come, too?"

"No, sweetheart. I have to stay in New York for a while. Miss Lily is having her baby after Christmas, so someone needs to help her."

"I'll miss you, Miss Kathleen," George said, before taking her hand in his.

"I will miss you, too, George, but now you are learning your letters, you can write to me. I will write you back."

"You will? That will be great," George replied happily. "What are you going to ask Santa for, Miss Kathleen?" the child asked. Kathleen wasn't sure how to answer without ruining the magic.

"Yes, Miss Kathleen, what are you going

to ask Santa for?" Richard asked, as his eyes danced in amusement.

Kathleen gave Richard a look before turning her attention to George. "Santa is for children only, George. He doesn't take requests from adults."

"Why not? You said he was magical, and Doc Richard said he can grant wishes." The little boy was resolute in his belief. She knew he wasn't going to let the subject drop.

"Yes, he can, but…"

"George, you have to believe in magic for Santa to work, and maybe Miss Kathleen doesn't," Richard added.

"But, Miss Kathleen, you have to believe in magic, else it won't come true. You got to try. Will you try? Please?"

"Yes, George. Now look, you are next." Kathleen stared at the young boy working beside Santa. He looked familiar, but she couldn't place him. He looked up, probably due to her staring, but there was no sign of recognition in his face.

CHAPTER 36

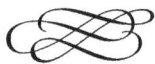

They moved closer, George thankfully now completely distracted by Santa.

"Your name?" the boy asked George.

"George. What's yours?"

"I'm Santa's helper," the boy replied, his haughty tone making Kathleen smile. He looked at her, causing her to quickly cover her mouth with her hand. She didn't want him to think she was making fun of him.

"You got a name?" George insisted.

"Kenny."

Kathleen took a deep breath. It was the

boy they'd been looking for. She didn't know what to do. What was the child doing working beside Santa? He wasn't dressed like an elf, so he couldn't be working for Macy's. Yet he definitely was close to Santa. Was Inspector Griffin mistaken? Did Kenny have a family the policeman didn't know about?

George climbed up on Santa's knee and told the man a little about himself. When he said he wanted a new family for Christmas, Kathleen had to wipe her eyes. She wished she had a magic wand and could make sure George got his happy ever after. She knew it was wrong to have favorites, but George held a special place in her heart. The six-year-old was like an open book. He loved everyone and everything and, as a result, was easily hurt. He had been luckier than most of the orphans in that he had a loving family who had cruelly been taken away from him. The child had grieved for his family but then, with the resilience of youth, had bounced back. He'd been lucky to have landed in the sanctuary, never having experienced the horrors of the streets of New York.

When George climbed down, Santa beckoned Kathleen to come closer, but instead, Richard took her place. "Forgive me, Santa, for butting in, but I need your help."

Santa eyed Richard warily, but at a quick whisper from Richard, his face turned into one, big smile.

"So, young man, you want something from Santa?"

The children from the sanctuary giggled, as Richard went down on his knees, as if pretending to be a child.

"Santa, I have been good, and I would like something really special, but I need your help."

"What do we think children, should we help him?"

The children roared yes, the noise of the crowd making the younger ones move closer to Kathleen. Her attention was fixed on Richard. What was he doing?

"Santa, can you ask Miss Kathleen Collins to come closer?" Richard asked.

"I will indeed. Children, is there a Miss Kathleen Collins in the crowd?"

The children roared their approval and pushed Kathleen to the center. They moved around her as if to prevent her from running away. She couldn't do anything but stare at Richard.

"Santa, I would like to ask Miss Collins to marry me. Do you think she will say yes?"

Santa pulled at his beard as he looked to her, his eyes dancing with laughter as he struggled to stay serious.

"Well, young man, you should really ask her and not me. I think Mrs. Claus might be put out, if I were to agree to marry again."

Everyone laughed, the adults at the joke and the children just because it was Santa.

Richard moved directly in front of Kathleen.

"Miss Collins, will you do me the honor of becoming my bride?"

"Yes," Kathleen whispered, hardly believing this was happening.

"Can I kiss the bride-to-be please, Santa?"

"I think you better, or your audience will be disappointed."

Richard stood up and drew her gently into his arms. She gazed up into his face, watching his lips, as they came down to meet hers. It was the most fleeting of touches, like butterfly wings grazing her cheek, but it was enough.

"I love you, Kathleen Collins. Thank you for making my Christmas special."

"Yes, Santa is magic," George hollered, much to everyone's amusement.

CHAPTER 37

*K*enny watched the lady carefully. He recognized her. She had lived next door to Mrs. Fleming. She had older brothers and a younger one, but he couldn't remember their names. He remembered she was kind, though, always smiling. She had known Mary. He had seen them talking a few times. He looked at Santa and wondered if he had brought the lady here today.

He saw the man kiss her and watched as her face went all funny before going bright red. Everyone was cheering, which drew even more people toward Santa's grotto. Kenny glanced around and then froze solid. Staring back at him was Lucky, and he didn't look happy. Kenny inched closer to Santa, but the old man was distracted by the couple in front of him. He moved closer still, until he was practically sitting on the man's lap.

"Kenny, what's wrong? Aren't you happy for these folks?" Santa asked him, putting his arm around Kenny's shoulders. He was shaking, and he knew Santa could feel his bones rattling. Lucky kept coming and motioning at Kenny to come to him. Kenny couldn't move, even if he'd wanted to. Apart from the fact Santa's arm would stop him, his legs were frozen to the spot. Santa stared into the crowd, too, but Kenny didn't know if the old man could see very far even with his glasses perched on his nose.

"Kenny, you're shaking. There is nothing to be scared of. I'm here, and this young woman works with the lady I was thinking of. Kathleen Collins, let me introduce you to my friend, Kenny."

The lady stared at him, and he saw the recognition in her eyes. She seemed glad to see him. She whispered something to the man who had kissed her, before bending down to Kenny's level.

"My word, Kenny, but you have grown so tall, I didn't recognize you. Do you remember me? We met a few times when I lived near Mrs. Fleming."

Kenny nodded, his thumb stuck firmly in his mouth now. Mary hated him sucking his thumb, said it was for babies, but sometimes when he was really scared, it helped. Now he was terrified. What was Lucky going to do with all these people around?

CHAPTER 38

"There you are, kid. I've been looking for you all day. I should have known you would have come to see Santa. I hope you haven't been getting into mischief," Lucky said loudly, forcing his way through the crowd.

"No, he hasn't. He has been a great help. Who are you?" Santa asked, his tone as cold as the weather outside.

"I'm his brother. Our ma is going to leather the both of us for being out so long. Come on, Kenny, let's get you home."

Kenny shrank back from Lucky's arm,

causing the lad to give him a hard stare. He inched closer to Santa and Kathleen. Kathleen pushed her way in front of Kenny, glaring at Lucky.

"I don't know who you are, mister, but you aren't anything to do with this child."

"Says who? He's my brother, and we need to go home. Now!" Lucky made a grab for Kenny but missed, due to the man who had kissed Kathleen putting his hands on Lucky and dragging him back a few steps.

"You nearly knocked my fiancée there. You need to calm down," Richard insisted.

"Get your hands off me. Kenny's my brother, and I am telling ya now, we are off."

"Kenny is not your brother. He grew up beside me, and I knew his sister and his parents. The only brother he had was a babe who died before his first birthday. My name is Kathleen Collins, a friend of Inspector Griffin, and I have been searching for Kenny for days. I am taking him home with me."

Lucky glared at her for a few moments. Kenny thought he would wet himself, he was so scared.

"Over my dead body, missus," Lucky said. "You keep your beak out of things, if you know what's good for you."

"How dare you threaten a decent, young woman, you despicable young man!" a man who was waiting to see Santa with his two young children said disgustedly.

Kenny almost grinned, as Lucky realized there were more than a few adults glaring at him. He hoped it meant the man would leave. But then he would go home. To Jack. He would hurt his dog. Kenny couldn't let that happen.

"Lucky has been looking after me, miss. I best get home with him, or his ma will kill both of us. Thank you for your kindness, Santa."

Kenny moved toward Lucky, who grasped his shoulder in a painful vice-like grip. He tried not to make a sound, as he figured Lucky would make him pay for it later.

But he hadn't reckoned on Kathleen.

"Let go of that child immediately. You, call the police," Kathleen ordered a member of the staff, who had been watching the scene unfold. "Kenny Clark, you are coming home with me. Inspector Griffin is very worried about you, him being an old and dear friend of your mother."

Ma didn't know Inspector Griffin, least he didn't think she did. Miss Collins was telling lies. Why?

"Kenny, we are going now to get Jack. He will be upset if you don't come home with me," Lucky countered.

Kenny couldn't let anything happen to Jack. He looked at Kathleen and then turned to leave with Lucky.

"The dog will run away, you'll see. Kenny, don't leave with him," Kathleen begged.

"Nobody is leaving. The police will be here shortly."

Kenny stared at the man who had asked Kathleen to marry him. He looked very angry, but he was looking at Lucky, not him. Was Kathleen, right? Would Jack run away if he didn't come back with Lucky?

"Keep him then," Lucky shouted, as he pushed Kenny into Kathleen and her friend before bolting. Kenny watched, as a couple of men tried to stop Lucky, but he slipped past them easily. It was all over in seconds.

"Kenny, you are safe now. You'll come home with us," Kathleen said. "Come along children. We will come back to see Santa another day."

"Why don't I come to the sanctuary to see you, miss?" Santa suggested. "I could do with catching up with Lily, I haven't seen her in some time."

"Thank you, Santa. We would love to see you. Perhaps you can help us finish decorating our tree," Kathleen answered, holding her hand out to Kenny.

Kenny hugged Santa. "Thank you for

helping me," he whispered, as the red-suited man hugged him back.

"Be good, Kenny, and may all your dreams come true."

KATHLEEN COULDN'T BELIEVE the afternoon. Between Richard proposing and finding and, just as quickly, almost losing Kenny again, it was very memorable. Thankfully, the other children were very understanding about Santa. The fact he was coming specially to see them at the sanctuary helped, but with the exception of George, the other children had lived on the streets. They knew the danger. They might not understand what Lucky wanted with Kenny, she wasn't sure of that herself, but they knew enough to know he was in danger. Richard hailed a couple of cabs to take them home. He rode in one with the younger children, while Kathleen rode in the other with the older ones and Kenny, who wouldn't let go of her hand.

"Do you think Jack will be all right?" the boy asked her.

"Yes, Kenny, I do. I think he will come looking for you. He will go to Granny Belbin. We can send word to her to tell her where you are. For now, I want to get you to safety."

"What did Lucky want with me?"

"I am not sure, Kenny. Perhaps Inspector Griffin will be able to tell us. But you can take that worried look off your face. You are safe with us. I promise."

Kenny looked at her with such trust. She promised nothing would hurt him again, not while she was around.

CHAPTER 39

*O*nce back at the Sanctuary, Kathleen ensured Kenny had a wash and something to eat, before tucking him into bed. He was sharing with George and some of the other younger boys.

"Why hasn't Jack come?"

"Give the dog a chance," Kathleen said. "I will send my friend Mike over to Granny Belbin to explain where you are. She was worried sick about you. She will keep an eye out for Jack."

"Thanks. I loves that dog. Lucky, he tried to kick him, but he missed. I don't like him, but his sister Angel … she was nice. She saved me from some other boys, and she fed me, too."

"Kenny, did any of them say why Lucky wanted you to go to Macy's?" Kathleen asked him.

A tear rolled down Kenny's cheek, making her pull him to her into a big cuddle. "It's okay, sweetheart. You are here now. Nothing will happen to you."

"He said he would take me to see Santa. Mary said Santa was magic, and he could make things happen. I thought Santa would find Mary and Ma and send them back to me."

Kathleen's heart broke in her chest. The poor child didn't understand Mary was dead and his ma had killed her. Now wasn't the time to explain what had happened.

"Did Angel or Lucky mention anything else?"

"Angel didn't want to go away. She said her aunt would make her wear girl's clothes —she dresses like me. She owns these clothes, or at least she did. She is bigger now."

"Why were they going away?" Kathleen asked.

"Something to do with someone called Priest or at least I think that's what his name was. Eastman," Kenny mumbled, as sleep overtook him. Kathleen caressed his hair until the child was fast asleep. She heard someone whisper her name and looked up to see Richard. They hadn't spent a minute alone since he'd proposed earlier, but for now, that would have to wait. She was terrified for Kenny.

"How is he?"

"Richard, he is so scared. He said Santa was going to find Mary and his ma. And he said Lucky and his family were going to run away from someone called Priest Eastman, but I'm guessing he meant Monk."

Kathleen watched Richard's reaction, as his face paled, his expression matching hers.

"Monk Eastman?" Richard repeated the name feared by many.

"I'm afraid so, yes. It seems from what little Kenny said, the family he had stayed with were on the run from Eastman."

"We should speak to Inspector Griffin. Last thing Lily or the sanctuary needs is to become a target of the Eastman gang. Oh, my darling, I want to take you and run from here this second. Not very manly of me, is it?"

"I think you're wonderful. I can't believe you asked me to marry you in front of all those people. It was beautiful."

"Well, it was supposed to be, but I didn't even get to give you the ring. But we can finish that another time. This is more important."

"Richard, you understand what these children mean to me. George and the rest of them are wonderful, and I want to help them find homes, but Kenny... I can't explain it, but he's different. I feel closer to him for some reason. Maybe it's because I knew Mary, although we weren't close."

"He might remind you of your little brother. But don't worry, come downstairs, and we will send for Inspector Griffin. Bridget and Carl are helping Cook tidy up. Charlie arrived a little while ago with Lily."

"Lily is out this late?" Kathleen asked.

"I asked them to contact Bridget, so I could ask her permission to ask you to marry me. She was very excited and wanted to be here when we came home to congratulate us."

Kathleen couldn't believe she had been doubting his feelings, while he was doing his best to propose in the correct manner. Bridget had known all along and hadn't mentioned anything. Her sister was good at keeping secrets.

"You wrote to Bridget?" she queried.

"Yes, well I sent her a telegram a while back. Could have saved money, if I had known she would arrive in New York before Christmas," he joked, before taking her hand. "I wanted to ask you so many times, Kathleen, but I was worried you would think I was pressuring you. I know I said I would wait however long it took, but it seems patience is not one of my virtues."

She stopped him talking by kissing him. His arms circled around her, as he drew her closer.

CHAPTER 40

When they arrived back downstairs, Inspector Griffin was already waiting with her sister, Carl, Lily, and Charlie. Mini Mike and Tommy were there, too. Kathleen could see by their facial expressions, they were very worried.

"You heard about Kenny?" she asked, conscious she was stating the obvious.

"Tommy sent a boy to find me. He said Kenny was involved with the Eastman gang. This is more serious than we imagined," Inspector Griffin said, his serious tone matching his facial expression.

"I don't know how involved Kenny was," Kathleen said. "From what he said, I think the man who took him to Macy's had fallen out with Eastman."

"Lucky Spielman and his two brothers worked closely with Monk Eastman until recently. In fact, many said Lucky was the obvious replacement should anything happen to Monk. News on the street is Monk is out for blood, and that can't be good for Kenny," Tommy clarified.

"You know what happened between Monk and Lucky?" Inspector Griffin questioned Tommy.

"One of the guards on a building under Monk's protection got killed, but I'm not clear on how Lucky got involved. Might have been a fight. The Eastmans have closed ranks. It's difficult to get answers, but we'll keep trying. How's Kenny?" Tommy asked, obviously changing the subject.

"Worried about Jack, but I told him the dog would probably get back to Granny.

Can you get word to her he is here? But best tell her not to let anyone know," Kathleen replied.

Tommy nodded.

"I will have to talk to Kenny. What did he tell you?" Inspector Griffin asked Kathleen.

"He said a girl called Angel protected him from some boys and brought him back to her house where she fed him. He had to have a bath, which he was very put out about."

Lily and the others smiled, as they knew from experience how much the street kids hated baths.

"He said Angel was kind, and she gave him new clothes and fed him. She also told him to run away from her brothers. But Lucky heard her, and he stopped Kenny."

"Did Angel say why Kenny should run?" Inspector Griffin asked.

"No, but Kenny said she seemed frightened. He said Lucky was nice to him the night before but changed in the morning. He said something about his big, blue eyes and blonde curls making women weep. Kenny wanted to know why people would cry by looking at him." Kathleen could let her imagination run away with reasons why Lucky would want to make an impression on women, but none of them were good.

"Sounds to me like Lucky intended on using Kenny as some sort of decoy. I better speak to the Macy's security men and make sure they are on the watch for the gang. A bit hard to miss given how tall the boys are," Inspector Griffin said.

"You got to get Kenny away from here, Miss Kathleen. Monk Eastman is a bad 'un. Not just for Kenny but for the sanctuary, too," Mike spoke up, his neck coloring. Kathleen knew he hated being the center of attention.

"Yeah, we dealt with the gangs before, but Monk, he takes things up a level." Tommy looked furious. "He is making a name for himself, and it ain't because of his charms and good looks."

"But I thought you worked with someone in his gang, Tommy?" Lily asked, causing Tommy's neck to turn red.

"You shouldn't be saying stuff like that, Miss Lily. That was our secret."

"Tommy, we are among friends. I thought everyone knew you had an agreement with the gangs to help take the little ones off the street."

Kathleen looked between her two friends. This was the first she had heard of any agreement. Glancing at Bridget's expression, her sister was just as surprised as she was. She thought they did everything they could to avoid getting involved with the vicious gangs.

"You work with the gangs? But I thought they wanted the children to join them? Raise their own brand of cutthroats and pickpockets," Richard asked, his disdainful expression earning a look of rebuke from Tommy.

"Tommy has what we call an understanding with certain gangs. They don't want the really young children, as they consider them a burden. The older kids they can train to become members of the gang, but some are not suited, such as those whose arms don't work properly, or they got something wrong with their legs. Those kids, the gangs let us take and bring here or drop them at the Christian Aid Society. Brace was working with the street gangs since the start, but he never told nobody. It wouldn't have shown him in a good light with some rich folks."

Kathleen stared at Mini Mike. That was the most she'd ever heard him talk.

"The gangs helped us save a lot of kids over the years. They aren't all bad, you know. A lot of what they do, they do to survive," Tommy protested.

"Yes, Tommy, we know. But that's because we have seen first-hand what the streets are like. For those born in the large, brownstones, I guess they see things differently," Lily hastened to reassure him.

"Even the police have been known to use the gangs. That right, Inspector?" Tommy's challenging tone alerted Kathleen. She turned to the inspector who was looking distinctly uncomfortable.

CHAPTER 41

"What's he talking about?" Kathleen asked.

"Don't glare at me like that," Inspector Griffin pleaded. "It wasn't my idea, and I have never condoned it."

"Condoned what?" Kathleen pushed for an answer.

"There have been some allegations made about the police," the inspector explained. "They are accused of returning runaway gang members to the gangs rather than helping the kids leave New York," Inspector Griffin said, staring at the floor.

"But why would they do that?" Bridget whispered, clearly shocked. "It's certain death. The gangs don't let anyone leave. Not voluntarily."

"Yes, I know, but not everyone thinks of these kids as being human beings. It's not right, but that's a fact of life," Inspector Griffin said decisively. "Anyway, we need to concentrate on the problems we can fix, and we have two big ones at the moment. Kenny has brought the Eastmans' attention to the sanctuary which isn't good, and Kenny himself needs protecting."

"Kenny will be safe here. We won't let anyone touch him," Tommy said firmly.

"I am not doubting you, Tommy, you know that. But this is bigger than just Kenny. We don't know how desperate Lucky and his brothers are. We need to find out more about the falling out," the inspector said. "I can try my sources, but we both know you are more likely to be told than a copper."

Tommy acknowledged the inspector's

words with a nod and a glance at Mike, whose face remained unreadable.

"Inspector Griffin, we will do all we can to get you the information we need. I will go visit this Angel," Kathleen added.

"You can't," Richard contradicted her.

"Yes, I can."

"Kathleen, I forbid it," Richard said. "It is far too dangerous."

She glared at him. "This is my job, and I won't ask anyone's permission to help a child. If you don't know that already, perhaps you don't know me at all."

Kathleen didn't mean to be sharp, but what she had learned over the last half hour had sickened her. She regretted taking her frustration out on Richard, but at the same time, she meant every word. From what Kenny had said, this girl Angel had helped him despite the risk. That was all Kathleen needed to know. She had to help the girl.

"We will go with you, Miss Kathleen. You cannot go to see Angel alone," Tommy insisted. "Lucky is nasty on his own, never mind when the three brothers get together."

"I strongly forbid you from going, Kathleen."

Kathleen looked at Richard sadly. "I think you should go home. We will talk when we have both calmed down a little."

Richard looked as if he was going to argue but then thought better of it as he turned away. He said goodbye to the others. Charlie offered to see him out. Kathleen didn't move from her chair.

CHAPTER 42

"*D*o you know where the family lives, Tommy?" Kathleen asked, as if nothing had happened.

Tommy blinked rapidly before shaking his head. "I will find out. I'll come back tomorrow. Mike, we should go check on Granny. Maybe stay with her tonight just in case."

Kathleen could have kicked herself. She hadn't given any thought to the danger Granny Belbin may be in. What if Kenny had told Lucky and his family about her protecting him and giving him shelter?

They would assume she would know where he was.

"Take a basket from Cook with you. Granny won't accept charity, but she can't refuse to share a meal with you. Can you come back tomorrow morning?" Kathleen added.

"Yes, Miss Kathleen," Mike said, while Tommy added his thanks.

Inspector Griffin followed the men out, saying he, too, would make inquiries and return in the morning. Charlie left the room to check on the children, leaving Kathleen, Bridget, and Lily alone by the fire.

"Kathleen, come sit here beside me," Lily said, patting the sofa. "I know you are upset, but Richard was only reacting to what he heard. You know he never lived in the tenements and has only ever enjoyed a comfortable lifestyle. He probably had no idea until today just how dangerous the lives of the children can be."

"He deals with poor children in the hospital," Kathleen protested.

"Yes, but those are children whose families take them to the hospital, not orphans like our kids," Bridget said, in a soothing tone.

The hair on Kathleen's neck stood up. She hated when Bridget used that tone with her. It made her feel stupid.

"Give him a chance, please," Lily said. "He only said what he said because he loves you."

"He does? He has a funny way of showing it," Kathleen retorted, although she knew Richard was just worried. It annoyed her he had thought he could order her around, but she knew his actions showed he was worried about her. She shouldn't have reacted so harshly.

"Yes, darling Kathleen, he does," Lily said. "He went to a lot of effort to ask Bridget her permission to ask for your hand. He is a wonderful, young man, if a little authoritarian, but we can smooth those edges."

"I know you hate it when you think I am talking to you like a child," Bridget said. "But if you look inside your heart, you will know we are right. The man is head over heels in love with you."

Kathleen stared into the fire considering what Lily and Bridget had said. It was normal for a man to want to protect the woman he loved. She remembered her da looking out for her mam. And Carl and Charlie would do anything for Bridget and Lily.

"You weren't very fair with him, were you?" Lily asked gently.

"No, I guess not. I was angry. I never heard that about the police before. Can you imagine how much it took for those kids to try to escape the gangs, only for the very people who should have protected them to hand them back? Why, Lily?" Kathleen asked.

"I can't answer that," Lily said. "But it

isn't Richard's fault or even Inspector Griffin's fault. No matter where you go in life, there will be those who don't treat others properly. We can't worry about them. All we can do is try to do the best we can for the children who come our way."

"You are so wise, Lily," Bridget said.

"Me? I don't think so. Charlie will tell you how often I have ranted and raved about things I can't control. I think I have grown a little more patient, but that depends on the mood I am in. Anyway, speaking of my husband, here he is back to collect me. Are the children all right?" Lily asked Charlie, as he walked into the room.

"Yes, they are all asleep," Charlie reported. "Kenny did ask for Jack, so I told him you were going to try and find him. He fell back asleep. I think the poor kid is exhausted."

"After everything he has been through over the last few days, that's hardly surprising. How will he recover?" Bridget asked.

"He will be given time and lots of love

and understanding. You will find him a wonderful family. Now you should try to get some sleep. You, too, Kathleen. The next few days are bound to be very busy."

"They are," Kathleen agreed. "I completely forgot about the meeting with the sponsors. They want to hear updates on some of the children and also how the plans for the new farm school are progressing."

"I can go to that for you, if you like, Kathleen. Carl knows a lot about it," Bridget added.

"Thank you, sis," Kathleen said gratefully, realizing just how tired she was.

"It's a pity Charles Brace won't be here to see that school. I think he would have liked the idea. When is Father Nelson coming over to discuss it?" Lily asked.

"On Monday. The Children's Aid Society is responsible for the setup of the school, but they have agreed to us placing some boys there. Father Nelson believes it will be a good way to get more farm placements for the boys from Hell's Kitchen, as at least they will have some experience after they finish in the school." Kathleen quickly brought the others up to speed.

"It sounds like a fantastic idea, but for now, Mrs. Doherty, you need to get home and get some rest. Between the new baby coming and those rascal twins of ours, you are worn out," Charlie said, helping his wife to her feet.

"Charming, next you will be telling me I look old," Lily replied, teasing her husband.

Their antics made Kathleen smile. The love between this couple was obvious to everyone. Charlie adored his wife, and he was protective. She felt guilty, as Charlie's actions reminded her of Richard. She had been too hard on him. She would need to apologize tomorrow.

"Goodnight, Kathleen, sleep well and good luck tomorrow. Don't go near Angel's house without Tommy and Mike. You promise?" Lily put her hands on Kathleen's arms and forced her to look at her as she spoke.

"Yes, I promise, Mom!" Kathleen replied. "I won't do anything stupid." She kissed Lily on both cheeks and did the same to Bridget and then closed the door behind the two couples. Leaning against it, she felt completely overwhelmed by what she had learned that evening, together with what it meant for the coming days.

CHAPTER 43

Kenny woke the next morning wondering where he was. George jumped on him, tickling him. He pushed the boy off and looked around in the hope that Jack had returned when he was sleeping, but that was silly. Jack didn't even know where he was. He got dressed quickly and went down to look for the lady who had helped him the day before. She said she would try to find Jack. He didn't want to leave his dog with Lucky and his brothers any longer than he had to.

. . .

"MORNING, Kenny, are you hungry? Cook made pancakes," Kathleen greeted him, once he'd made his way downstairs.

Pancakes were his favorite, and his belly was rumbling, but Kenny knew he should go look for Jack.

"I need to find Jack." He followed Kathleen into the kitchen, all thoughts disappearing, as he stared at the mound of pancakes sitting in the middle of the table. Cook turned at the growling sounds coming from his stomach.

"I think someone is hungry this morning, young man. Do you like maple syrup on your pancakes?"

Kenny stared at the pancakes, "Yes, please."

"So sit yourself down then, child." Cook directed him to a seat, tempted as he was, since Jack could be in danger.

"I have friends out looking for Jack, so why don't you sit and eat, and then we can make some plans," Kathleen said, as if reading his mind. "Does that sound good?"

Kenny nodded. He didn't know what she meant by plans, but he would do anything for this lady. She had taken him away from Lucky.

George showed him where to get a plate and cutlery, and then the cook put three, big pancakes on his plate. Three just for him. This place must be like Heaven. He ate quickly, worried one of the other children would take his.

"Slow down there, Kenny, or you will be sick. There is plenty to go around. Cook will make more if you want them," Kathleen said, smiling as she ruffled his hair.

More?

"It's good here. They feed us real well, and we have a Christmas tree and all. Do you want to see it?" George said cheerfully, his mouth full of pancakes.

"I am sure Kenny would love to, but after breakfast and chores," Kathleen said.

Kenny groaned. He hated chores. Mary used to make him sweep up and go and find kindling for the fire. At the thought of his sister, his throat felt funny. He tried to force some pancakes down, but he couldn't. He pushed the plate away reluctantly.

"Are you full already?" Kathleen asked.

He nodded, not sure his voice would work. He wanted to be by himself in case he started crying. He thought he might, and he didn't want to be a baby in front of these kids. They might seem nice, but there were adults around. Who knew what they were like when they were on their own.

"Can you take your plate out to Cook please, Kenny? Then George will bring you to my office, so we can talk."

"Sure will, Miss Kathleen," George said. "Does that mean my chores are done?"

"Nice try, George," Kathleen replied, her eyes bright. "I think I heard Sheila say it was time to sweep out your bedroom today."

"Ah, man, I hate sweeping. I can never do it right, and she makes me do it again and again," George muttered under his breath.

"She? George remember your manners."

"Sorry, Miss Kathleen. Sheila makes me do it over."

"Sheila wants the place to look nice for when Miss Lily visits. Now go on, Kenny, and go through to Cook. She won't bite you."

Kenny picked up the plate and went in search of Cook. She was really nice, giving him a big smile and telling him she would cook him something nice for his tea. She didn't make any comment on him not finishing the food on his plate. His ma would have gone nuts. But he didn't want to think about her at the moment.

"You ready, Kenny?" George asked. "I got to go sweeping."

CHAPTER 44

*K*enny reluctantly followed George to what he assumed was Kathleen's office. He knocked on the door and opened it when he heard her voice. Once inside, he stood at the door, shifting from one foot to the other.

"Come in closer to the fire," Kathleen said. "It's nice and warm. Sit there on the sofa. One of my friends said he would call this morning, so he will join us soon."

"Inspector Griffin?"

"No, Kenny, a man called Tommy. He

knows Granny Belbin. I asked him to tell her you were safe. She was worried about you."

"She was kind to me. Not scary like I thought she would be," Kenny said. "Will Tommy have Jack?"

"I don't know, sweetheart, but I hope so. I think Jack is a clever dog and will find his way back to Granny's, don't you?"

"He will, if they let him."

KATHLEEN WANTED to hug Kenny tight and promise him everything was going to be fine, but she couldn't. She didn't know if Jack would make it back and certainly couldn't promise, even if he did, that Kenny would be able to keep the dog. She hadn't heard of an orphan being placed in a new home with an animal in tow. She hoped Tommy would arrive soon with good news.

"Kenny, do you remember where Angel

lived? Would you be able to tell me how to get there?"

"You're going to bring me back to them?" Kenny asked, suddenly nervous.

"No, sweetheart, of course not. I am going to see if I can help Angel. She helped you, didn't she? Maybe she needs a friend. Wouldn't you like me to ask her?"

He studied her face, as if debating with himself what the best answer would be. Kathleen waited for him to decide. It wasn't her role to tell him how to feel about things.

"I think she might need a friend, but I don't know if she'll leave her brothers. I don't think you should go alone. Lucky is already angry with you. He may hurt you, and I wouldn't like that to happen. You're nice."

She hugged the boy close, to thank him for his kind words but also to give her a minute to compose herself.

Her heartbeat drummed in her ears, but

she tried deep breathing to still it. She couldn't let Kenny know she was terrified. She didn't want to go anywhere near Lucky or his brothers, but she had to. Angel needed her help. She refused to leave the girl alone, especially after her kindness to Kenny.

"Thank you, Kenny, for being so thoughtful. I will be careful, I promise." Kathleen hoped her confident tone would reassure the child and was relieved her voice wasn't shaking, although her knees were. "I will bring Tommy and Mike with me."

"Good. Nobody would try anything with them two there, they're tough. Everyone knows that."

Kathleen acknowledged his words with a smile. Tommy and Mike may act tough, but both of them had huge hearts. If she told anyone what they had done over the years to help Lily, she doubted anyone would believe it. They looked like rough characters, but that was part of why they were so successful. They could blend in with the people from the toughest neighborhoods and find out who needed the most help.

CHAPTER 45

Kenny was able to give her a good idea of where Angel lived. She promised the little boy she would thank the girl for looking after him if Angel decided to stay with her brothers. Then Tommy and Shane arrived and with them, Jack.

"You found him!" Kenny squealed. "Jack, come here to me. Who's a good boy? Are you okay?" Kenny rubbed the dog over with his hands, as if checking him for injuries. Jack couldn't stop licking Kenny. He ran around him and jumped up and down, until Kenny picked him up in his arms. Even then, the dog kept licking his face.

"He seems fine to me, Kenny. Was he at Granny's?" Kathleen asked.

"Yeah, turned up whining yesterday evening," Tommy confirmed. "She said she nearly did him in herself during the night, as the mutt wouldn't stop crying. Kenny, she told you she sends her love, but she said you can keep Jack here with you. He messed up her floor again."

"Jack, you bold dog. You know you shouldn't do that. Granny's old. It's not fair on her to make her clean up."

Even though he was scolding the dog, Kenny was still patting his head, and Jack was still licking his face and wagging his tail. Kathleen, Shane, and Tommy exchanged smiles before Tommy beckoned her outside. Shane followed Tommy out of the room, his dour expression causing her mouth to go dry. She knew her brother, that he had bad news and was afraid to share it with her. What had he gotten himself mixed up in now?

"Kenny you stay here with Jack, and I will be back in a few minutes."

"Sure," Kenny replied, as he sat on the sofa with Jack sprawled over his knees.

Kathleen closed the door behind her, so Kenny wouldn't hear what the adults spoke about.

"Lucky's been seen at the tenement. He may have set the dog loose so he could follow him. Mike stayed with Granny. We've persuaded her to move for a few days," Tommy explained.

"Are you going to bring her here? There's plenty of space."

"No, but thank you, Miss Kathleen. It's better she is somewhere near. She don't like being made a fuss of, and the kids might be too much for her. She loves Kenny, but she is wary of lots of children. She says they make too much noise, but between you and me, I don't think she can handle any more goodbyes. She has looked after lots of kids in her lifetime, and they've all moved on."

Kathleen nodded in understanding. "What do you know about Lucky? Were you able to find out anything about his feud with Eastman?"

Tommy nodded, before checking again that the door was closed. He glanced at Shane who sighed before explaining,

"Seems Monk believes Lucky was skimming the profits, taking a percentage for himself. Everyone does it, and usually Monk turns a blind eye, but Lucky got greedy. A man got killed, and the place he worked in was under Monk's protection. Monk thinks Lucky made him look bad. So Monk wanted to teach him a lesson and show him who was boss, only Lucky's brothers got involved too. They didn't like their brother being picked on. Monk is furious."

"How do you know all this?" Kathleen

asked, although she didn't really want her suspicions confirmed. Why was Shane mixing with gang members? Hadn't he come close enough to prison?

"Monk trusts Shane," Tommy said quietly. "Before you go jumping to conclusions, Miss Kathleen, there are some things you don't know."

"And that's the way it will stay," Shane said, meeting her gaze. He stood straighter.

"Shane, don't be like that? I can't but worry you are in over your head."

Tommy looked at Shane before turning to Kathleen. "It was Shane who rescued the dog. He followed Lucky to the tenement, guessing what his plan was. He intercepted him before Lucky got to Granny. Granny owes him her life."

"She does?" Kathleen's high-pitched squeak caused Shane to frown harder.

"I ain't a kid, Kathleen. I know how to defend myself. These are the streets I grew up on."

Kathleen didn't contradict him, but she looked to Tommy.

"We still got a problem with Lucky. I didn't kill him, only scared him off. He may still come after Kenny."

"Why Kenny?" Kathleen asked.

"Lucky thought, if he got some money together, he could make it sweet with Monk again," Tommy said. "He was heard bragging of how much he made in Macy's. Seems he was showing Kenny off as his younger brother, and when the ladies were cooing over Kenny, Lucky was picking their pockets."

"Still, he can't have made that much," Kathleen said, surprised women would be carrying much cash. She thought they would be more likely to charge their purchases to their accounts.

"Well, he thought he did okay. I think he had ideas for other schemes involving Kenny. But you stole him away. Now he ain't happy. Monk ain't happy either, but we are doing our best to focus his rage on

Lucky, not the sanctuary. Leave that to us. Kenny should leave New York. Angel too."

"Is Angel involved with Monk as well?" Kathleen asked.

"No, of course she isn't. Monk won't take Angel."

Shane stood with his arms crossed across his chest.

"Easy, Shane, your sister isn't the enemy."

"I got to be somewhere else. Keep that kid inside," Shane ordered, before he opened the front door. He was gone before she could say anything.

"Shane's frustrated Lucky got away." Tommy looked to Kathleen, "Angel's safe from Monk for the moment, but we think it's only a matter of time before she becomes a pawn. Monk has a reputation for the services he provides. He could use a young girl."

Shocked, Kathleen took a step back from Tommy as if she could distance herself from his horrible words.

"Tommy, they're her brothers."

"You quit being that naïve as soon as you got fired from Oaks's place. You and I know the way the world works. The sooner we can get Angel away from those brothers of hers, the better."

CHAPTER 46

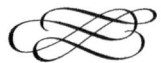

Kathleen knew Tommy was right. She wasn't as naive as she had been, but some things still shocked her. Lily said that was a good thing, as it showed she still had her decency and sense of morals. Her brother being mixed up with the gangs worried her, but she had to focus on Angel for now. Shane had made it clear he didn't want Kathleen's help.

"Kenny knows where she lives. He gave me some good directions. Will Mike come with us?"

"Me and Mike will go. You stay here,"

Tommy said.

Kathleen put her hands on her hips as she gave him a piece of her mind. "Don't you start ordering me around as well. I am going with you. Angel won't trust you guys together. At least we have a chance she will trust me."

"You are as stubborn as Miss Lily, Miss Kathleen," Tommy said, pretending to back away from her in fear.

"I consider that a compliment."

They were interrupted by the door opening behind them as Kenny popped his face around it.

"Sorry, Miss Kathleen, but I think Jack has to go. He's crying again. Thank you, Tommy, for bringing him home."

Kenny edged past them, the dog following at his heels. They watched as they made their way to the kitchen, waiting until Kenny was out of earshot.

"We will go this afternoon if that suits you," Tommy said.

"Yes, the sooner the better, as you said."

"I best go and get Mike. Someone else will look after Granny."

"Tommy, was there any news of Kenny's ma?" Kathleen asked.

"Nope. Nobody has heard or seen her. I reckon she went for a swim in the Hudson."

Kathleen shuddered as the door closed behind Tommy. She didn't agree with what Mrs. Clark had done, but she wouldn't wish suicide on anyone. She went back into her office to make sure the fire was safe. She didn't want any accidents—life in the sanctuary was dramatic enough. Sheila soon interrupted her.

"Cook would like to see you. It seems Kenny thinks the dog is going to live here. Cook ain't having any of it." Sheila wrung her hands in the apron at her waist. Kathleen knew the girl was afraid of Cook who could become very hot and bothered but, at heart, was a lovely, kind woman.

Kathleen rolled her eyes, wishing Bridget were feeling better, but Richard had confined her to bed rest for the next two days. She could do with Mrs. Wilson's help, but she had yet to return from her extended visit with her sister. She had left shortly after Maura and the other girls had robbed the sanctuary and had yet to return. Lily thought she would eventually, but Kathleen had her doubts. In the meantime, she would have to deal with Cook and her fear of animals.

She managed to strike a compromise between Cook and Kenny. Jack could stay at the sanctuary so long as he had a bath and never went into the kitchen or dining area. He had to be locked in Kenny's room when Kenny went downstairs to eat. Kenny had balked at this at first, but when given the alternative, which was for Jack to make his home in the shed, he soon agreed to it. Jack hated his bath, and they ended up with more than one child soaked to the skin, but it cheered Kathleen up to see everyone smiling. Even Cook had come to take a peek at the dog getting washed. Maybe with time, she would grow fond of Jack.

CHAPTER 47

Soon it was time to leave to search for Angel. Kathleen told Kenny to stay with George and pay attention to Sheila, who would look after the children until her return. She took him outside with Jack, so Jack could relieve himself. While they were waiting, she spoke to Kenny.

"Under no circumstances are you to go outside, do you hear me?"

"But what if Jack needs to go again?" Kenny asked.

"He can go in the backyard. Kenny, you

have to stay in the sanctuary. Do you understand why?"

Kenny looked at his toes for a few seconds before raising his fear-filled eyes to her.

"Lucky might come looking for me to take me back to his house."

She knew then he'd been listening to her conversation with Tommy and Shane. She only hoped he hadn't heard how worried they were for Angel.

"Yes, darling, he might," Kathleen said. "But you are safe in here. Nobody will come into the building. So promise me you will stay with the other children."

Kenny kicked at the snow. Jack came running back to them, and so he picked him up and held him close.

"I promise. Will you tell Angel I said thanks?"

Kathleen bent down and gave him a hug. "I will, darling. Now let's get you back inside before Jack and you freeze."

She repeated the conversation to Sheila,

making sure the girl knew the children were to remain inside, regardless of how much they begged to go and make snowmen. She hated the fear in the girl's eyes, but every member of the staff had to be on alert. From what Tommy had said, Lucky wasn't a man to be trifled with.

CHAPTER 48

Inspector Griffin wanted to accompany them, but Tommy had declined, saying it might spook the brothers as well as Angel.

"We don't want any trouble, so it's best you stay back," Tommy said. "We can send someone, if we need you."

Inspector Griffin didn't like the idea, but it was hard to argue with Tommy.

"Did you find any sign of Kenny's ma, Inspector?"

"No, Kathleen. She seems to have just vanished. Nobody has seen her, or if they have, they aren't talking. Father Nelson is going to have the funeral for Mary on Monday. Are you coming?"

"Yes, I will bring Kenny with me. I think Granny Belbin, Mr. Fleming, and a few of the neighbors from the tenements are going too. I assume you will be there?" Kathleen asked.

"Yes, but in an official capacity. There are some who think the mother might show up. Catholic guilt is a powerful emotion." Inspector Griffin looked at his hands, taking a couple of seconds before he spoke again. Kathleen felt sorry for him, guessing this was part of police work he hated. "It is always awful attending a young person's funeral, but being Christmas makes it worse, doesn't it?"

"Yes, Inspector, it does. But we will all look after Kenny. What are you and your wife doing for Christmas dinner? You are more than welcome to join us at the sanctuary, if you wish. We have plenty."

Kathleen would have smiled at the expression on the man's face but for their earlier conversation. He looked like a child invited to a party, only to find he couldn't go.

"I would love to, thank you very much for your kindness, Kathleen, but the wife always goes to her sister's. It's a long family tradition."

"Family is important, especially at Christmas. I will ask Cook to pack up a basket of her mince pies and maybe a small pudding, if you don't think that would offend your sister-in-law."

Inspector Griffin' eyes lit up. "Oh, it would be lovely. Cecily might be offended, but her husband and I would be delighted. I know I shouldn't say this, as it is rather disloyal, but my wife and her sister were not blessed when it comes to domestic talents."

Kathleen smiled, knowing that, despite his wife's failings as a cook, the man loved her dearly.

"Kathleen, we got to go," Tommy called.

Kathleen picked up her skirts and

walked faster to keep up with Tommy's long strides. They would have gotten a cab, but the cab drivers were too nervous to drive down to where Angel lived. Maybe she should have listened to Richard after all, but even as the thought crossed her mind, she knew she couldn't have stayed home. Not when a child might be at risk.

CHAPTER 49

*I*t didn't take long to reach the street Angel's family lived on. Tommy stopped walking and asked Mike to stay with Kathleen while he went to see if he could see anyone inside. They waited, Kathleen blowing on her knitted mittens in an effort to warm up her chilled hands. She looked around the street with interest, having never been in the area before. It wasn't as poor as the tenements, as someone had tried to clean up the street a little. The lower levels of the properties were stores of all kinds with the living quarters above. Some stores were boarded up, but others appeared to be thriving.

"Come on, Miss Kathleen. Tommy is calling us," Mike said, taking her arm. She walked slowly, trying to quell her nerves. She reminded herself that she would be safe with Mike and Tommy. Then she spotted Shane.

"What are you doing here?" she demanded, not bothering to hide her anger. He had stormed out of the sanctuary to come here. Was he working for Monk?

"I have business with Lucky. What are you doing here? You should have stayed at the sanctuary. This is men's work."

Kathleen could have fallen over her own mouth. How dare he say something like that? She was about to argue, but a look from Tommy stopped her.

"You two can deal with your personal stuff in your own time. We got a job to do. I think Angel might be inside alone," Tommy said.

"I'll check," Shane offered.

"Let Tommy," Kathleen said. "He knows what he's doing."

"I said I would check. You can't tell me what to do, Kathleen, so shut up."

She did, more out of surprise than anything else. Shane was usually pleasant with her, but then life on the streets had made him toughen up.

Mike held her arm, as if to say "let him go," so she kept silent. She watched as Shane crossed the street, looking around him carefully before he slipped up the stairs and knocked on the door. The girl opened, and it was clear she recognized Shane.

They spoke for a few seconds. It was obvious from the way the girl kept looking over Shane's shoulder she wasn't happy about what he was saying. But he gestured to them to come over anyway.

"Angel, you know Tommy and Mike. This is Kathleen, my sister."

"Your sister?" Angel asked, clearly comparing Shane's ragged appearance to Kathleen's neatness.

"Yes, she scrubs up well, doesn't she? She lives in Carmel's Mission. You heard of it."

Her response was to hit Shane hard on the arm. "I ain't stupid. Of course, I heard of it. It helps the kids from the street and some women who have disgraced their families. The boys said it was an ex-whore who started it."

"Lily is a whole lot more than that," Kathleen responded sharply, earning herself a hard look from Angel. She softened her tone. "Lily has been a good friend to my family. To all of us, including Shane, isn't that right?" She directed the question to Shane, who shuffled from one foot to the other before nodding his head.

"What do you want?" Angel asked. "My brothers will be back shortly, and they won't be happy to see you here."

"Kenny is safe," Kathleen told her. "We wanted to thank you for looking after him."

"I didn't do nothing." The girl kept looking out the window, her fear evident.

CHAPTER 50

Kathleen's heart went out to her, because underneath her hard exterior, she could see the girl was very thin and obviously not dressed for the winter conditions. As she glanced around the small rooms, she saw they were clean and tidy, if rather spartan.

"Kenny told us everything you did for him, from saving him from a group on the street to taking him here and feeding him. He said you warned him to run away from your brothers."

"I never did. He's lying. The boys wouldn't hurt a child."

Despite her indignant tone, it was clear Angel didn't believe the words she was saying. She refused to meet Kathleen's gaze.

"We don't got much time. We know the boys are in trouble with Monk. That puts you in danger. You have to come with us," Tommy insisted.

The girl backed away, glaring at Tommy.

"I ain't going nowhere. The boys will sort it out with Monk. They been working with him for years. It was all a misunderstanding."

Shane stepped closer to her. "Angel, stop it. You know Monk don't do misunderstandings. Your brothers are in deep, and you'll pay the price."

"Don't start that again, Shane. You don't know what you're talking about."

"I do, and you know it's the truth," Shane said. "Lucky needed Kenny, but he lost him. He lost everything but you. You're his ticket out of this mess, and he ain't afraid to use you."

Angel paled, her face a mixture of emotions. She stared at Shane. "He wouldn't. I'm his kid sister. He always looked out for me. Ever since Ma died."

"He has? That's not what I been hearing. Or seeing. When was the last time he ever did anything nice for you?" Shane asked. "You know Axel is the one that keeps him in line, but now Lucky might be too big for Axel to do that. Axel has his own priorities. He's been wanting to get out of New York for years."

"He doesn't mean that. He jokes about going to live with Aunt Rachel, but we all know he's lying."

"No, he ain't, Angel. He's got a girl, and she's real religious. Her father goes to the synagogue, and word is he won't let Axel near his daughter unless he starts going too."

"Axel in a synagogue?" Angel balked. "Don't make me laugh, Shane."

Kathleen saw the girl was conflicted, struggling to deny what Shane was saying, although it was obvious it made sense to her at some level.

"Angel, why don't you come with us and stay for Christmas. Let this all pass over, and then you can come back," Kathleen suggested.

"I don't celebrate Christmas."

"I know that." Kathleen's sharp response earned her a look from Tommy. "What I mean is, just come and stay for the celebration part. We won't force you to go to mass. Kenny would love to see you, as would Jack."

Angel's face grew animated. "He got Jack back? He loves that dog, nearly died protecting him. If Lucky's boot had caught him up higher, he would have."

Kathleen had no idea what the girl was talking about, but it didn't sound good. Tommy glanced out the window and gestured toward the door. They needed to hurry up.

She glanced at Shane who was staring at Angel, adoration fighting with annoyance in his gaze.

"Angel, listen to Kathleen, please. She knows what she's doing. You will be safe in the sanctuary."

"I can't go. I can't leave them. They need me."

"No, they don't. Can't you see? Lucky will sell you down the river just like that." Shane snapped his fingers before moving to put his hands on Angel's shoulders. "I ain't trying to hurt you, but you got to see the truth. It ain't safe for you. It never was, but you really annoyed him the way you looked out for Kenny. He blames you for the fact the kid got away."

He moved his hands down her arms, but the gesture made her shrink away from him. Kathleen saw his face turn red as he pulled Angel's sleeve up, revealing nasty bruises on her arm.

CHAPTER 51

"He did this, didn't he? Don't lie to me," Shane said, holding her shoulders.

"Shane, stop shouting. That's not going to solve anything." Kathleen pulled her brother away from Angel. Turning to the girl, she pulled her sleeve down and drew her to sit on the sofa beside her. "Angel, you can't let your brother treat you like this. We can keep you safe if you come with us now."

"I can't," Angel repeated. "They're my family."

"That's about to change, Angel," Shane

interrupted, but Angel didn't acknowledge him. Kathleen hid her surprise, as she had to convince Angel to leave with them. The bruises on her arms were more proof her brother wasn't going to keep her safe.

"Did Kenny tell you about his family?" Kathleen asked her softly.

"He said he'd lost them and was going to ask Santa to find them. He said the cops told him his sister was dead, but she wasn't."

"His sister Mary was fourteen years old, just slightly younger than you are now. She died at the hands of Kenny's mother, her mother. Some families don't treat their loved ones the way they should be treated. You know Lucky is going to get worse. You can't stay here, not if you want to live."

Angel didn't reply, the look of shock on her face speaking volumes. She obviously had believed Kenny's sister was going to be found. It amazed Kathleen that the girl could be so innocent yet seem so tough at the same time.

"Listen to her, Angel. I've been trying to get you away for the last year. You can't keep livin' like this. If they don't kill ya, they will sell you to Monk. You know that. Don't be stupid," Shane said sharply.

Kathleen saw Angel's eyes widen as the girl retaliated.

"Who are you callin' names. I live in a house. What are you offerin' me? A bed on the street? Until someone better comes along? My brothers told me about men like you."

Kathleen couldn't believe what she was hearing. Shane was even more involved with this girl than just fancying her. A Jew? Not to mention the sister of some heavy-hitting gang members. How had they even met, never mind gotten to know each other so well?

"Angel, you know that isn't what I want. I want us to be together. For always, but you aren't old enough yet. I want you to come to Riverside Springs with me. You will be safe there. I told you before that's what I want. I ain't leaving New York without you. But I won't let you live here anymore. You're comin' with us, whether you like it or not."

Angel scrambled away from Shane as he moved nearer. Kathleen stood too, the girl coming to stand behind her as if Kathleen would protect her. Kathleen knew her brother wouldn't hurt Angel. No matter what else he had done, he was always wonderful with children and wasn't going to lift his hand to a woman. Especially the woman he claimed to love.

"Shane, you can't kidnap her. That's a crime," Kathleen chided her brother.

"I don't care. I ain't leavin' her here," Shane protested, his facial expression telling Kathleen it was pointless trying to argue with him. She glanced at Tommy.

"We got to go. Won't be long until one of your brothers shows up," Tommy said.

"Too late. They're here now," Shane said, glancing out the window, his face a hard mask.

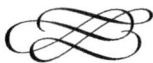

CHAPTER 52

*A*ngel turned whiter than the blanket of snow on the rooftops. Shane moved to her side as she whimpered.

Kathleen guessed the girl wasn't even conscious she had made a noise, so great was her terror.

"What are we going to do, Tommy?" Kathleen asked.

"You stay inside with the girl. Shane, you better stay too. If they catch sight of you, it will only inflame things. Mike and I will deal with this. You keep her indoors."

Tommy gestured to Angel. Kathleen nodded. "Be careful."

Kathleen held her breath as her two friends left the rooms and walked down the steps out onto the road. She watched as the brothers stopped dead in their tracks, catching sight of the boys coming out of their home. She felt Angel step up to the window beside her. The girl was trembling.

"Axel and Haviv. I don't know where Lucky is," the girl murmured.

Kathleen's hopes raised. Out of the three brothers, Lucky was the worst. Maybe Tommy could reason with this pair. They watched the foursome for a few minutes. They appeared to be arguing but were too far away for them to hear anything.

"Come on girls, out we go." Shane gestured toward the back of the room. "We can't sit here and just wait."

"Shane, you heard Tommy. He said to stay here," Kathleen protested.

"Tommy doesn't tell me what to do. It's too dangerous. Lucky will be here any minute. Come on, get out before it's too late."

Kathleen wanted to hit her brother. He wasn't helping at all. "I am not leaving. Tommy said to stay here. Angel is staying with me."

Shane rounded on her, his eyes wild.

"Why are you always so stubborn? You have no idea how dangerous her brothers are. They don't think twice about killing someone who gets in their way."

Kathleen stood straighter, squaring her shoulders back. She wasn't scared of Shane. He would never strike her; she knew that.

"I don't care. Tommy knows what he is doing, and he said to stay here. You aren't thinking straight. You are too close to this problem. Why didn't you tell me you were involved with Angel?"

Shane looked away from her. "You're not my ma."

Kathleen's temper finally broke.

"Don't you speak to me like that. I spent weeks crossing the country trying to find you, and this is how you repay me. Going behind my back and not giving any care to your safety. Getting mixed up in things you shouldn't." She wished she could put the words back in her mouth as Angel turned on her.

"I take it that means me. You don't think I'm good enough for your brother?" Angel spat, fire coming out of her eyes.

Kathleen reached out for the girl, but Angel stood back.

"No, Angel. That isn't it at all. I am not sure he is good enough for you, given his current occupation. He lives on the street, as you said. He is mixed up in goodness knows what." She turned her attention back to Shane. "Michael sacrificed his freedom so you could have yours, and this is what you do?"

Shane gave her a look, which made her wonder what he'd been hiding.

"You always thought you knew it all, didn't you, Miss Goody Two-shoes. You haven't a clue what I have been doing since I got back."

"So, tell me," Kathleen screamed at him, losing all control. She glared at Shane with him returning her angry look. Angel's intake of breath got both of their attentions.

"What is it?" Shane asked.

"Lucky."

CHAPTER 53

The dread in Angel's voice made Kathleen feel guilty. She shouldn't be fighting with Shane when the girl beside her needed help. Shane and she could deal with their issues later. This girl's safety was their reason for being here. Kathleen glanced out the window. The day in Macy's, Lucky had been very tall and good looking, and it was easy to see how he charmed the women. But not today. He was scowling, and it twisted his face up. Maybe Shane was right and they should leave through the back. But it was too late. Lucky was already halfway up the steps, his brothers, Tommy, and Mike following behind him. Shane pushed Angel and Kathleen behind him, standing in front of them as the door opened.

"I should have known you had something to do with this. I thought we had got rid of you years ago," Lucky snarled.

"You touch her again, you piece of dirt, and it will be the last thing you do. She's coming with me," Shane said.

"What are you going to do with her? Get married?" The sneer on Lucky's face said it all.

"In time. But for now, she is coming somewhere safe."

"You can't take her anyway. She's under my control," Lucky said.

"Actually, it's my control. You forget I am the eldest."

Kathleen watched another brother, who wasn't as tall as Lucky but seemed to be more muscular. He had an ugly scar on his face, but for some reason she sensed he was more even headed than his brother. Was this Axel? The one who wanted out of New York?

"You all should be ashamed of yourselves for the way you treat your sister. Her arms are covered in bruises, and I guess there are others we can't see. How big and brave you are to beat up a girl," Kathleen said contemptuously to the brother who had just spoken.

"I don't know who you are, lady, but I ain't put a hand on any woman." Axel's denial rang true.

"You might not have, but he has. Show Axel your arms, Angel," Shane instructed.

"This true, Angel?" Axel asked quietly, his brown eyes glued to his sister's face. Kathleen watched Angel. Would she tell the truth?

"Show him, Angel." Shane's tone was gentle yet firm.

Kathleen could tell that he really did care a lot for her, despite their youth. Shane was only a year younger than she was, but the life he had lived to date had made him grow up fast. She guessed Angel was the same. Although only fifteen, she looked older.

Angel pushed the sleeves back slowly, her eyes on the floor. Axel's disgusted reaction told Kathleen he hadn't known of his brother's abuse.

"Shane, go and take Angel with you. Everyone out," Axel ordered.

"But…" Angel said.

"Angel, I will find you. I know who to ask," he glanced at Shane before fixing his stare back on Lucky. "I got unfinished business with our brother. Everyone out."

Axel's tone meant business. Kathleen led the way, Shane grabbing Angel's coat from the hook at the door and pushing her after Kathleen, with Tommy and Mike following behind.

"Come on, let's get a cab and get out of

here before he changes his mind." Tommy took charge of the situation.

"What will he do to Lucky?" Kathleen asked Tommy, careful to keep her voice low, so Angel wouldn't hear her.

"I don't think you want to know," Tommy replied. "Let's get you home."

CHAPTER 54

ommy hailed a cab, and soon they were driving back to the sanctuary. On arrival, Richard came out to meet them, followed closely by Charlie and Carl. Kathleen was surprised to see her brother-in-law, as she thought he would be back at Lily's looking after Bridget.

"Where is Bridget?" Kathleen asked him.

"She stayed behind with Lily," Carl explained. "She said she was taking a nap, but I think Laurie and Teddy may have had other ideas. How did it go?"

"Good now we are home. Come inside. I

have to make a guest comfortable, but I will be down soon."

Carl and Charlie turned back to go inside, but Richard stood waiting, an uncomfortable expression on his face. She walked over to him.

"Richard, I—"

"Kathleen, I'm sorry. I shouldn't have presumed like that yesterday. I just wanted to keep you safe."

"I know, and I'm sorry too. I guess I can be a bit stubborn at times."

"More than a bit, sis!" Shane said, as he walked by holding Angel's hand.

"Who is that?" Richard asked.

"That's Angel. She has some nasty bruises on her arms, and I suspect elsewhere."

"Does she need a doctor?"

Kathleen looked at the man she loved. He really did care about people. "I don't think so, but I'll ask her. She is a pretty tough cookie."

"Is she going to stay here now?"

"Yes, for Christmas, but I am not sure after that. One brother beat her, and the other just told us to leave while he dealt with him. I guess you could say their family is rather complicated right now."

"I am just glad you are safe. Young Kenny was very worried about you. He's waiting for you inside."

Richard offered her his arm to escort her into the sanctuary. Cook had already made tea and gingerbread cookies. Kathleen asked Angel to come with her to find Kenny who was sitting in his bedroom with Jack.

"I brought a friend back to see Jack and you," Kathleen said.

Kenny looked up, his sad little face lighting up when he saw Angel.

"You came. They said you would, but I wasn't sure. Thank you."

Jack nearly tripped Angel up, as he ran around her legs. Laughing, she sat on Kenny's bed and let the dog sit on her knee, while she put her arm around Kenny. Kathleen saw that the action hurt her by the way the girl winced, but Angel didn't let on to Kenny.

"You look good, Mouse, better than you did when you came to my house."

"I got new clothes, and Cook feeds me. A lot! You should taste her pancakes. Who are you?" he demanded when Shane walked in the door.

"Shane is my friend and Kathleen's brother," Angel explained.

"Oh. Well, don't get any funny ideas. I'm marrying Angel when I grow up. She's my friend." Kenny's tone told the others he was serious.

Kathleen hid a smile as Shane and Angel exchanged a loving look.

"Sure thing, Kenny. But you have to grow into a good man," Shane said. "She deserves a husband who treats her right."

"I know that." Kenny looked down his nose at Shane, making Kathleen choke on a giggle.

She withdrew from the room leaving

the three of them to chat freely. Inspector Griffin had sent a note to say he would come by in the morning to speak to Angel. Kathleen wondered if the girl knew how much danger she was in.

Shane followed her out.

"Kathleen, I'm sorry about the way I spoke to you. You didn't deserve that."

"Angel has to leave New York. Are you really prepared to go with her? I thought you wanted to stay here."

"I came back for her. I met her years ago, but at first, we were just friends. Being sent away made me realize I loved her."

"But you were…"

"Don't tell me we were kids. We stopped being children the day Mam died. I know how I feel, and Angel feels the same."

Kathleen laughed, making Shane scowl. "Don't look at me like that Shane. You can't tell me you are not a child one minute and sulk like one the next. I'm sorry. I didn't mean to belittle your feelings for Angel. Forgive me?"

He nodded, but, as she continued to stare at him, he smiled.

"Do you want to go back to Riverside Springs?" she asked.

"Yes, I liked it there. I came back to New York for Angel and for something else."

Dying to know what else he was involved with, she waited for him to expand, but he stayed silent.

"You seem to know what you are doing. Don't look at me like that. You are my brother, and I care about you. I don't like you being on the wrong side of Monk Eastman or anyone else."

"You leave Monk to me and the boys. Just promise me you will look after Angel," Shane said. "She needs a friend."

"If you are going to marry her, she will get more than she bargained for. Have you told her what sisters are like?" Kathleen joked, giving her brother a quick hug. He hugged her back before dropping his hands, his face red with embarrassment.

"I best get back before Kenny grows up and marries my girl."

Laughing, Kathleen walked down the stairs to find Richard, but he had already left.

CHAPTER 55

The next morning, Inspector Griffin arrived, and as Kathleen had guessed, he did want to speak to Angel. Shane refused to leave her side, so he joined the meeting, as did Carl. Lily and Bridget were at home resting.

"Thank you for seeing me," Inspector Griffin began. "Angel, Lucky turned up in Bellevue last night."

The color drained from Angel's face. Kathleen could understand her shock. No matter what he had done, he was still her flesh and blood.

"Will he be alright?" Angel asked.

"He'll live. He got beaten up pretty bad. You wouldn't happen to know who hit him, would you?" Inspector Griffin asked, his gaze landing on Shane.

"Shane came back with us when we brought Angel here, and he didn't leave till late. He couldn't have hurt Lucky," Kathleen answered, then turned red as she realized she had made him sound guilty. Inspector Griffin hadn't accused him of anything.

"I wanted to hurt Lucky, Inspector. After what he did to Kenny and to Angel, but I didn't touch him. I swear."

"But you know who did, don't you, Shane?"

Shane didn't answer. Angel took his hand and moved closer to him. They stood together, their expressions telling everyone in that room they would never talk.

Inspector Griffin turned to Kathleen. "I believe you were there when Lucky came back to their home."

"Yes, Inspector, but he looked fine and

healthy when I left." Kathleen wasn't about to speculate, although she was certain it was Axel who had beaten up his brother. As far as she was concerned, the sanctuary didn't need to get involved in a war between gang members, whether they were related or not.

"So, nobody in this room can help with my investigation?"

"Sorry, Inspector, but it would appear not. What does Lucky say?" Kathleen asked.

"He says he didn't see them," Inspector Griffin said. "A group of men jumped him."

"Well, I guess you got to take his word for that," Shane replied, a little too smugly for Kathleen's liking. She saw the Inspector felt the same.

"Can I get you tea and something to eat, Inspector?"

"No, thank you, Kathleen, I have to get on. It's been a busy weekend."

"Any sign of Kenny's mother?" she asked.

"None. What will you do with him?"

"We think it would be better to get him out of New York. After the incident with Lucky, we feel he would be safer if he lived elsewhere. I guess you won't have any objection to that?" she asked.

"None at all. It's a wonderful idea. I best get off. Shane, I'm sure I will be seeing you around."

Shane didn't reply. Kathleen showed the inspector out and then came back into the room where Shane and Angel were arguing.

"I have to see if he is all right. He's my brother."

"You can't. You know what will happen. You got to stay out of this and leave it to Axel," Shane said, before turning to Kathleen. "Can you make sure she stays here? I got to go out for a while."

"Where are you going?" Kathleen asked, although she guessed it was something to do with Angel.

"Out."

Kathleen knew he wouldn't give her any details. "Be careful and don't be long."

He smiled, but it was a tight smile and did nothing to mask the worry in his eyes. "I'll do my best. Keep her here."

And then he was gone.

CHAPTER 56

The day dragged by, although Kathleen tried to keep herself and Angel busy. If she had a penny for every time the girl looked out the window, she would be rich. She eventually asked Angel to go into the office and wrap some more presents.

Carl had gone home to check on Bridget and then returned, bringing Charlie with him.

"Any news?" Charlie asked as he came in.

"No, and I am going out of my mind. I

will kill Shane myself when he gets back. What's he thinking?" Kathleen asked.

"I guess he knows what he is doing. He's been working and living on the streets for a while now," Charlie replied.

"Has he joined Eastman's gang?" she asked.

"No, Kathleen, of course not. He isn't in any gang. He's been helping me, actually. He wanted to live alone. He didn't tell me why, but now we all know the reason."

"But how has he been helping you, Charlie?" Carl asked.

"He's helped us clear up a few inquiries. He can go places I can't. Don't stare at me, Kathleen. It wasn't my idea. It was his. He said he had to pay the community back for the bad stuff Michael and he had done. He's part of the reason we got so many orphans in the last year. He works closely with Tommy and Mike."

Kathleen sat down, thinking of all the bad thoughts she'd had about Shane over the last few months. He had been doing good, and she'd assumed the worst.

"Don't look so guilty, Kathleen. It suited Shane's work if you were annoyed with him. You didn't exactly hide your reaction, and neither did Bridget. It made what he was doing more credible."

"Does Bridget know now?" Kathleen asked.

"Since last night, but she isn't happy," Charlie said. "In fact, she's furious with me. I left her with Lily, who isn't too happy with me either, but I swear Shane was going to do this anyway. At least by working with me, I could protect him where possible. At least that was the theory. This thing with Lucky has me worried."

"Charlie, please don't take the blame. Shane has always followed his own path or Michael's." Kathleen smiled weakly, trying to hide just how worried she was. Charlie Doherty didn't deserve to feel bad. The man had only done what he thought was best for everyone.

"Shane will be back soon. Tommy and Mini Mike won't let anything happen to him," she added with more confidence than she felt.

The hours went by with no news from anyone. Angel had wrapped every present, and they were all piled under the tree. Tomorrow was Mary's funeral. Only after that could they start joining in with the Christmas spirit and only then if Shane arrived back safely.

Night fell, and there was still no word. Carl and Charlie returned home to their wives, leaving a frantic Angel and Kathleen to endure a very long night.

"Angel, try to get some sleep. We can't do anything until tomorrow. I will see Inspector Griffin at the funeral. Tommy and Mike should be there, too. I might get word."

"I will come with you," Angel said.

Kathleen was taken aback. She didn't think Jews went into Catholic churches.

"I know I may not be welcome, but I will

sit at the back. I want Kenny to know I am there," Angel said.

"Of course, you would be welcome. I was worried about your own people, not ours. Father Nelson welcomes everyone, regardless of what religion they practice. Kenny needs all the friends he can get."

Angel went to bed around one in the morning. Kathleen worked on some paperwork in the faint hope someone would come, but, after falling asleep twice on her desk, she gave in and went to bed. She prayed harder than ever before that her brother would be returned to her.

CHAPTER 57

Kenny woke up early. Today was the day he had to go to church and say goodbye to Mary. He didn't want to go, but nobody would listen. They all said he had to. They said it was what Mary would want, but he didn't believe that. She wouldn't want him to be scared, and the thought of seeing her in a coffin scared him half to death. Jack whimpered beside him.

He crept downstairs quietly, but when he went into the kitchen, Angel was already sitting at the table talking to Cook. Both had red eyes, as if they had been crying, but neither of them knew Mary, so they couldn't be upset about his sister.

"Kenny, would you like pancakes?"

"No, thank you, Cook. I ain't hungry."

"Are you sure? I could make them extra sweet just how you like them."

Kenny shook his head. He wasn't hungry, but instead, he felt ill. He sat at the table as Jack jumped up on Angel's lap. He glanced at Cook, but she didn't say a word. Angel fed Jack some of her breakfast. Judging by her full plate, she wasn't feeling too hungry either.

Angel looked tired as well as sad. He figured she must be worried about her brother. He'd overhead he was in the hospital, although he wasn't supposed to be listening, so he had to pretend he didn't know.

"You look sad," he said, hoping she would tell him about it.

"Do I? I just had some bad dreams,"

Angel said. "How are you feeling? Are you ready for today?"

He wanted to say yes, but he couldn't lie. Instead, he stared at the table.

"Someone told me you were going to sing a song. Is that true?" Angel asked.

"Yes, Father Nelson said it would be okay. He said I could sing a Christmas song. Mary loved Christmas. We never had a tree or nothin', but she always wrapped up a present for me. She liked me to sing 'Away in the Manger', so I thought I would sing it for her today. If I can. I tried upstairs to practice, but my voice sounds funny."

Cook sniffled loudly behind him. She was crying again. He didn't like crying women, so he climbed down off his seat and went looking for George. The other boy didn't cry much either, well, not in front of people. He cried into his pillow at night when he thought everyone else was asleep. George had told him about his mom and dad and how they died of some disease.

They sounded nice. Why did nice people have to go and die?

He kicked at a toy left on the floor. It splintered into pieces, and then he felt really bad. It was George's small fire truck, the one he usually kept under his pillow. He picked up the pieces quickly before anyone saw him. He didn't want to get into trouble, and he didn't want to upset George. Today was a bad day already, and they hadn't even gotten to church.

BRIDGET HELPED Kenny out of the cab, but he walked up to the door of the church alone. His knees were shaking. "One foot in front of the other, one foot in front of the other." He repeated the mantra under his breath, ignoring all the people staring at him. He didn't want to cry; he had to be brave. To make Mary proud.

CHAPTER 58

The church was crowded with people of all ages. Once inside, his feet wouldn't move. He looked up, shocked by how many children sat in the pews. Mary had always been kind to the little ones. He spotted Granny Belbin all in black. She looked older somehow but not scary anymore. Angel smiled as his gaze caught hers. She'd told him she'd sit in the back, as some people might object to her being in the church. Why would they care? Angel was his friend. He wished he could sit at the back with her. But Bridget had explained he had to represent his family, to honor his sister. He didn't want to honor Mary. He wanted to see her, feel her arms around him, and have her pick him up and take him away from this place.

He tried to move, but he couldn't. Frozen to the spot, he gulped back the tears. A larger, soft hand took his.

"Shall we walk up to the front together?" Bridget asked.

He gripped her hand. She was really nice, kind like her sister. He liked her a lot, and she liked dogs, which made him like her even more. She had explained Jack had to stay home, as he wouldn't be able to go to church. She said he wouldn't sit still and may scare people by running around. But she had brought him a big bone to chew on, so Jack was happy. Kenny was glad for his dog, but he wished he was able to hold him. It would make this easier. He kept his eyes averted from the coffin and focused on Father Nelson. Bridget had explained for him to do that, but she had also reassured him there was nothing to be afraid of. Mary was already in Heaven and looking after him. She wasn't cold or hungry anymore. Instead, she was happy and smiling all the time. He liked to think of her that way.

The mass lasted for ages. He knew bits and pieces of the Latin from when Mary had dragged him to church before. He stood up when the others did and kneeled down and sat just like everyone else. Then it came time for him to sing.

He walked up to the altar where Father Nelson had told him to stand. He faced the people, but there were so many, so he looked for Bridget. He sang to her, pretending she was Mary. He sang his heart out, and when his voice got all funny, he just kept going. Bridget kept smiling at him, her eyes looking very bright. She squeezed him tight when he finished and came back to sit beside her. She smelled really nice, of roses or some other flowers. He didn't mind at all that she cuddled him close. In fact, he liked it.

CHAPTER 59

athleen didn't pay as much attention to the service as she should. She kept looking around to see if she could see Shane or the boys, but none of them appeared to be in the church. Although it was difficult to tell since the building was packed. Mary had been a popular girl, but that wasn't the sole reason for so many being here. She knew many believed Mrs. Clark would show up, and they didn't want to miss that event. The killing of a child by her own mother had set the community on fire with people speculating over the reasons why. She'd heard more than one person blame Mary, as if the girl had done anything to deserve the way her life had ended.

Granny Belbin set the record straight a number of times, as she spoke of the girl who mothered her brother and protected him at great cost to herself. The old lady wouldn't hear a word against Mary and rightly so. Kathleen wanted to get her alone to ask her what she knew about Shane, but she couldn't get near her in the church. Afterward, the crowd seemed to swell, as the procession headed to the graveyard. She saw Bridget cuddle Kenny as the coffin was lowered into the ground. The boy threw a single flower into the grave and then turned, sobbing into her sister's knees. Bridget took his hand and walked him away from the graveside. There was no need for him to be there any longer.

Finally, she spotted Tommy. Kathleen made her way through the crowd slowly, as everyone seemed to want to speak to her.

Most wanted her to pass on their condolences to Kenny, but some wanted information she didn't have. She was polite but firm as she continued to where Tommy was standing.

"Where is my brother?" she demanded, as she got close enough.

"I don't know."

"What? You were supposed to be looking after him."

"Keep your voice down," Tommy urged. "People are looking."

Kathleen tried to suppress her temper. The graveyard wasn't the place. She followed him to a small café.

"I swear, I was watching him, and then a fight broke out, and everyone ran. The coppers were out in full force. I don't know if he got arrested or got away. I thought he would show up today," Tommy said.

"Where's Mike?" Bridget asked.

"With your doctor, getting patched up. He got hit on the head by a rock. He's fine now, but it was a bit of a mess."

"Richard was with you?" Kathleen couldn't hide her disbelief.

"No, we took Mike to him. We couldn't take him to Bellevue, as the cops could have picked him up. It got real nasty out there. There's a rift a mile wide in the Eastman gang. Monk is cracking down big time, and I think Shane may have got caught in the crossfire."

CHAPTER 60

athleen took a large gulp of tea while she tried to contain her rage and anger, not just at her brother but at men in general. When would they learn that fighting didn't get anyone anywhere?

"Where do we look next?" she asked. "We've got to find him."

"We don't go anywhere. You go home and leave this be," Tommy replied.

"Never. I'm not going to sit at home knitting while my brother is in danger. I told you before. I am a big girl. I think we should ask Axel."

"Are you nuts?" Tommy asked. "They don't like Shane."

"I think you're wrong. He let Shane take Angel. I think he's worth a try."

Tommy looked at her, but she couldn't make out if he thought she was right or completely nuts. He finished his tea and then stood up.

"Sure you want to do this?"

"Yes." She wasn't at all sure, and her legs were shaking, but she wasn't going back to the sanctuary without her brother. Bridget couldn't handle stress, and Angel was going out of her mind worrying. She didn't want the girl on the streets looking for Shane. Something worse could happen to her.

They called a cab and got out around the block from Angel's old house. When they walked up the steps, it was obvious someone had gotten there before them. The door was open. Tommy pushed Kathleen behind him as they walked inside calling for Axel. They didn't hear anything for a few minutes, and then they heard something from upstairs. Tommy told her to wait, but she didn't want to be alone, so she followed him.

"Axel," Tommy said, as he rushed to the man curled up in the corner. He had been badly beaten.

"We got to get him to Richard," Tommy said.

"Yes, and quickly," Kathleen said bending down so the injured man could hear her. "Axel, did you see Shane?"

Axel groaned.

"Have you seen my brother?" Kathleen repeated. "Please tell me. Angel is as worried as I am."

"Tell Angel I'm sorry. We are all sorry. Tell her to leave New York." The words sapped his strength, and Axel lost consciousness.

Tommy called a cab and took the three of them to Richard's office. Richard immediately set to work on Axel, leaving

Tommy and Kathleen to pace the room outside.

"What do we do now?" Kathleen asked.

"We got to wait and see."

"Do you think Shane did this?" she asked, although she didn't really believe Shane was capable.

Tommy shook his head, "No. Shane wouldn't have it in him. Not to leave someone in a state like that. Plus, Axel and he have an understanding. Or at least they did. Axel didn't want Angel involved with Shane, but he knew your brother wouldn't do anything to her. He knew they were in love."

Kathleen noticed his use of the past tense, but she refused to believe Shane was dead. He was hiding or in trouble, but not dead. Minutes passed. She paced the floor despite Tommy telling her to sit down, as she was making him nervous. What was taking so long? Was Axel dead? She couldn't tell Angel more bad news. And where was Shane?

After about an hour, the door opened, but instead of Richard, Mike walked in with a bandage around his head. She hugged him, careful not to touch his injury.

"I'm okay. Why are you here? I was looking for Richard." Mike glanced at Tommy.

"Richard's with Axel. He's hurt bad. No sign of Shane. Or the other brother." Tommy spoke in clipped tones. Kathleen knew he was worried about Mike but probably didn't want Mike to know.

"Haviv's gone," Mike said. "Last I heard, he was seen on a train to some aunt. Monk let him go. He isn't interested in him. He just wants Lucky."

"Good job Lucky is in Bellevue then," Kathleen said. She saw the look the boys exchanged. "What aren't you telling me?"

"He got out yesterday morning."

CHAPTER 61

Kathleen dropped into a nearby chair, her legs suddenly giving way under her. She wanted to cover her ears and pretend this wasn't happening. Just when she thought things couldn't get worse, they had.

"Kathleen, it doesn't mean anything. Lucky is in no shape to hurt Shane," Tommy said.

"You know that for sure? Why didn't you tell me?" she asked.

"I didn't get a chance to tell you. It was the funeral, and then we found Axel. We have people looking for Shane. We'll hear something soon."

Richard walked in without them even noticing. It was only when he spoke, she looked up.

"Shane is fine. He's asleep upstairs. I didn't know he was missing," Richard said, looking confused. "He needed some help, nothing serious. He has a broken arm, and he doesn't look too pretty, but he's fine. I thought you knew." Richard looked to Mike before looking back at Kathleen.

"When did he come to you?" Tommy asked.

"It was after you brought Mike in. I assumed he'd been in the same fight. I didn't send word, as you didn't tell me he was missing. I'm sorry."

"Can I see him?" Kathleen asked.

"Of course," Richard said. "Follow me."

"Doc, wait, how's Axel? Tommy said you were operating on him." Mike touched the bandage on his head.

Kathleen couldn't help but be thankful it wasn't this kind man on the operating table.

"He wasn't as lucky as Shane. I had to remove his spleen. The next twenty-four hours will be critical."

Kathleen followed Richard up the stairs to a room where Shane lay fast asleep.

"I gave him something to help him sleep. He was muttering about going back to find someone, but I thought it best he remain here. I may have given a slightly stronger dose of laudanum than required, but I had to keep him safe, and that meant here in the clinic."

Kathleen hugged him quickly, before going to her brother and kissing his face. He didn't move, but it was obvious he was breathing.

"Thank you, Richard."

"I'm sorry I didn't think of letting you know. It's been very busy here tonight. Tommy was worried the gang would come after Mike. So I didn't want to leave him either."

"Oh, Richard, why do these people have to tear each other apart? Do you think Axel will make it?"

"I don't know, but I hope so. He's young and strong and relatively healthy compared to his sister. They must have eaten first and given what was left over to her. She is skin and bones."

"Shane says he is going to take her to Riverside Springs to get her away from all this. Mrs. Grayson and the other women of the town will fatten her up," Kathleen said.

"And you? Will you be going too?" he asked.

She stared up at his tired eyes, his face white from lack of sleep. "No, Richard, not unless you go there too."

He bent to kiss her, but they were interrupted by a nurse calling for him.

"You should get back to the sanctuary and tell Angel what's happened. She can come here to see Shane and her brother, if he makes it. I have to go."

She watched him leave and then

checked on Shane once more. When she came downstairs, Tommy was gone, but Mike was waiting for her.

"We'll get a cab back to the sanctuary and pick up Inspector Griffin on the way. Tommy wants him to set up a guard on Carmel's Mission."

"Why?"

Mike looked uncomfortable.

"Mike, I asked why?"

"He's worried Lucky may go looking for his sister or Kenny. Both of them are in the same place. He just thinks it would be safer," Mike said.

"Where has Tommy gone?"

"I can't tell you that, but trust him. He knows what he's doing."

CHAPTER 62

athleen and Mike got a cab to the police station, where Inspector Griffin was stationed. Given Mike's injury and reputation, they decided it was safer if Kathleen went inside to ask for him, leaving Mike to wait in the cab.

"Kathleen, I didn't get to say hello yesterday," Inspector Griffin said, glancing at her and then taking another look. "How are you? You look, dare I say it, rather disheveled."

She glanced down at her clothes; he was

right. But she didn't have time to worry about appearances now.

"Inspector Griffin, you have to trust me. You've got to get a guard on the sanctuary now. Kenny and Angel could be in danger. I have a cab waiting outside. Can you come with us? Mike will explain it all on the way."

The inspector moved quicker than she expected for a man of his age. He ordered some of the beat cops to meet him at the sanctuary. He then grabbed his hat and followed her to the cab, doing a double take when he saw Mike.

"I'm guessing his injury is a part of the reason I am taking this trip?"

"Yes, sir." Kathleen quickly explained everything she knew and then left Mike to fill in the rest. The drive back to the sanctuary seemed to take forever. When they arrived, it looked the same as always. But she didn't get a chance to open the door. Instead, Angel came running out to greet her.

"Did you find him? Is he okay?" the girl asked, sounding panicked.

"Yes, I found him, but come inside. We need to talk. He's alive, but we have trouble," Kathleen told her.

Angel led the way into the office, where Bridget and Carl joined them. They quickly explained that Charlie was home with Lily, who was in bed after staying up all night.

"Shane is fine," Kathleen said. "Richard is looking after him."

"Can I see him?" Angel asked.

"Yes, but first you have to be brave, Angel. Your brother is at Richard's clinic too."

"Lucky?"

"No, it's Axel." Quickly Kathleen explained how she had found Axel.

"Did Shane do it?" Angel asked.

"No, Angel, at least not that we know of. You know he wouldn't be capable of doing something like that, unless you were hurt by someone. Axel didn't hurt you."

"No, it was Lucky," Angel confirmed.

"Which brings me to our next problem.

He is gone from the hospital. We don't know where he is, so there is a chance he might come here. Inspector Griffin is going to put a guard on the house."

"Here, but why?" Bridget asked.

"Because of me? I've put you all in danger. I have to leave." Angel stood.

"No, you aren't going anywhere. Shane would kill us if anything happened to you. Bridget, we don't know if Lucky wants Angel or Kenny. Maybe both of them," Kathleen explained.

Bridget paled and grasped Carl's hand.

"We will have the place watched twenty-four hours a day, seven days a week, and we'll make sure the guards all have a description of Lucky," Inspector Griffin outlined his plan. "Most of them have met him. You people will be safe, so long as you stay inside."

"I want to see Shane," Angel said.

"We know you do, and we do too," Kathleen assured her. "So Inspector Griffin will take us to him and leave his second-incommand to stand guard here. Bridget, you will have to make sure Kenny stays indoors, no matter what Jack wants to do."

Bridget nodded.

"Kenny and the other children will be fine," Carl said decisively. "Kathleen, go and get changed, and then you can go back to Shane. We will look after things here. Be careful."

Kathleen was never more grateful to anyone in her life. She ran upstairs to change before joining Angel and Inspector Griffin in a cab heading to Richard's office. Mike stayed behind, saying he would help Carl. Kathleen knew the gentle giant would protect the children and the sanctuary.

CHAPTER 63

The cab ride back to Richard's didn't take long. Richard greeted her with a hug and then took Angel to see Axel for a minute, as he was still out cold. Kathleen went straight to Shane's bed with Inspector Griffin. Her brother had woken up and was anxious to leave.

"I think you will have to cuff him to the bed, Inspector," Richard suggested, when Angel and he came in.

"That's not a bad idea, Doc," Inspector Griffin replied. "Shane, you want to tell me what happened to Axel?"

"I have no idea, Inspector, but it wasn't me. Axel is Angel's brother, and I wouldn't hurt him. He gave us permission to be together."

"I see," the inspector said. "Someone attacked him and left him for dead. Would you have any ideas about who that might be?"

Shane's expression suggested he did, but he wasn't talking. Angel sat on the edge of his bed, holding his good hand.

"Shane, I know the rule on the street is you don't rat on the gangs. But her brother nearly died. It's Christmas. Can't you give me something?" the inspector asked.

Shane glanced at Angel before answering, "I think you should look closer to home, Inspector."

Angel's face turned the color of Shane's bedsheets.

"No, he wouldn't. Axel's always looked out for us. All of us," Angel protested.

Shane took her hand.

"Lucky's in a bad way and probably behaving like an injured, wild animal, striking out at everyone. We both know what he's like. You can't be surprised," Shane said.

"How did you get injured, if it wasn't hurting Axel or Lucky?" Inspector Griffin asked Shane.

"One of your men did it to me, Inspector. I guess he thought I was part of a gang."

"One of my men? Tell me his name," the inspector demanded.

"I can't. There were a few of them, and I didn't stop to ask for their names. I will be fine. Doc said so." Shane turned his attention back to Angel. "We need to find Lucky. Do you have any idea where he might be?"

Angel stared into his eyes for a while before nodding. Turning to Inspector Griffin, "Do you have a pencil and paper? I can write the address for you. It's an abandoned warehouse. Just be careful. He isn't the only one who uses it as a hideout."

"Thanks, Angel." Inspector Griffin left. Angel collapsed against Shane in tears, making Kathleen decide to leave them to it.

She met Richard as she walked downstairs. "Is Axel any better?"

"Early signs are good, but he could use some prayers. Are they okay?" He nodded in the direction of Shane's room.

"They will be. Angel just gave Inspector Griffin the address where Lucky may be hiding. Shane thinks Lucky beat Axel up."

"I think so too, but he wasn't alone. He was too badly beaten himself. Inspector Griffin better bring backup."

Richard put his arms around Kathleen and held her close as she prayed for Angel, the inspector, and everyone else she cared for to be safe.

"Can you believe it will be Christmas Eve tomorrow?" he whispered.

"I know," Kathleen said. "I wish I felt more in the Christmas spirit, for the kids' sake."

CHAPTER 64

*K*enny was sitting on his bed when Bridget came to find him. He hid his face so she wouldn't know he'd been crying, but it was no use.

"Kenny, crying is good for us. It lets the sadness out. I cried when my mam and dad died, and I was older than you are now," Bridget told him.

"You're a girl."

"I sure am, but it doesn't matter. Does Jack ever cry?" she asked.

"He whimpers in his sleep. I think someone treated him bad before I got him.

But he is doing better," Kenny said, stroking his beloved pet.

"I think he is doing great, because he has someone to love him and care for him."

"I love him, and I don't want to lose him, but I will when I go on that train. Won't I?" He didn't look up as he asked but kept his gaze on the dog.

"Why do you think that?" Bridget asked.

Kenny debated whether to tell her the truth, but that meant admitting he had been listening, and he shouldn't have been.

"Did you hear the adults talking?" she asked.

He nodded.

"Did they say you might lose Jack?"

"They said a new family might not want a crazy dog. He's not crazy though. Well, I guess he is a bit, as he likes to chew up clothes. I don't know why. They don't taste good, but he likes it," Kenny said.

"I can't promise you a family will take you and the dog, but I think it could happen. Maybe if you said a prayer. I heard you already asked Santa for something, so maybe you could ask him for this too."

"I did, but they didn't come true. Mary didn't come back and neither did Ma," his voice choked, and, when she drew him against her, he didn't fight it. He let the tears fall. She stroked his hair as he cried, and it felt nice. She would make a great mom. He didn't know if she had kids, but it seemed like she would. She knew how to be around them.

He decided he could trust her.

"I did something bad," he whispered into her arms.

"What did you do, Kenny? Tell me. I promise not to be cross."

"I didn't mean to do it, but I kicked George's toy, the one he's been looking for. I tried to fix it, but I couldn't."

"If it was an accident, why didn't you tell someone?" Bridget asked.

"I didn't want anyone to be mad with me. I kicked it when I was angry. I asked Santa to bring me one, so I can replace it.

Do you think he will?" He risked looking at her face.

"I don't know Kenny, but he might. I think you should tell George, though. He thinks he lost it, and he feels bad about it."

"Will he still be my friend?" Kenny asked.

"Of course he will. He may be a little angry, but that will fade. You and George are good friends. Would you like me to come with you when you tell him?"

Kenny would, but he thought it would be better if he faced this on his own. He couldn't rely on her to always be by his side, although he wished, more than anything, she would be.

"I'll tell him, man to man. But thank you, Miss Bridget."

She hugged him in reply, and he stayed in her arms, never wanting the hug to end.

CHAPTER 65

$\mathcal{K}$athleen returned to the sanctuary alone, having left Angel with Shane and her brother. The girl wouldn't leave either of them, and Kathleen couldn't blame her. She would have done the same.

Bridget was waiting for her, so she quickly told her what had happened.

"I don't know whether to hug Shane or kill him," Bridget said, weeping.

"I know, but he loves Angel. Tommy and Mike said he does what he does to make up for the crimes Michael and he committed before they got sent west."

"What about Lucky? I hate the idea someone is watching us, especially the children."

Kathleen suspected it was one child in particular, but she didn't say so. She knew her sister had a soft spot for Kenny, but given her job, Bridget couldn't afford to get involved emotionally with the children. She had to maintain a distance in order to place them in homes.

A knock at the door scared them half to death. Sheila came in, closely followed by Inspector Griffin, his expression grave. He didn't meet her eye when he came into the room. She sat down, expecting bad news.

"Lucky won't ever hurt anyone again. Nobody is talking, but it's a toss-up whether he died because he left the hospital too early or someone finished him off. Anyway, I'll go and let Angel know. I just came to let you know the risk has gone."

"Thank you so much, Inspector Griffin. I wouldn't wish anyone dead, but I can't pretend to be sorry for him. He was a nasty man," Bridget replied, as Kathleen couldn't speak.

He was dead. The larger-than-life man she had met in Macy's. What could he have become if someone had taken him off the streets before he had gotten involved with a gang? It was pointless thinking like that, but sometimes Kathleen couldn't help herself.

Bridget saw Inspector Griffin out and then ordered Kathleen to bed in a way only an elder sister could. Kathleen felt guilty leaving her sister to cope, but she knew she needed some time away from everyone. She didn't think she would be able to sleep, but when her head hit the pillow, her eyes closed in no time.

SHE SLEPT FOR HOURS, and when she came back downstairs, she found Bridget and Carl with Sheila and the children. Bridget said Angel was up in bed and Shane was doing better. He was helping Richard watch over Axel. Richard was quietly confident Axel would make a full recovery and follow his brother to live with their aunt Rachel. Axel had given permission for Angel to remain at the sanctuary, and when she came of age, she was free to marry Shane.

Only then did Kathleen realize it was Christmas Eve and she had missed most of it. The children went to bed full of excitement for what the morning might bring.

CHAPTER 66

*E*veryone was up bright and early on Christmas morning. They went to mass first and then came back to have breakfast. Cook had made everyone's favorite. The men had a big fry with sausages, bacon, tomatoes, and eggs. The children could have that or pancakes, if they preferred. Kenny and George had a competition to see how many pancakes they could eat. Sammy, the runner Kathleen used regularly, came in to eat breakfast with them, and if anyone saw him stuffing food in his pockets, they didn't comment.

The present opening came after break-fast. George and the other children were almost jumping up and down with excite-ment. She saw Kenny looking several times at the door. Surely the poor child still didn't believe Santa was going to bring Mary back to life? How would she deal with his disap-pointment?

Clapping dragged her attention back to the events at hand.

Inspector Griffin went all red when he unwrapped his gift to see a brand-new pair of leather gloves.

"Just what I needed. Thank you, every-one," the kind man said, smiling.

"Cook insisted you take these as well, Inspector. As a special thank you for every-thing you did for us, including Angel and me," Shane said, pointing the man toward a large hamper of baked goods sitting on the table. "I would carry it for you, only my arm isn't cooperating."

"Doc said you were to take things easy.

You shouldn't try to carry anything," Angel ordered.

"I best get back to my wife. Thank you for everything. See you around, Shane. By the sounds of Angel's nagging, you will soon have a wife of your own," the inspector said, making everyone laugh.

"Actually, Inspector, you might not. I am going to see Liam and Annie in Riverside Springs. Angel is coming with me. We thought a change of scenery would do us both good."

Kathleen expected the inspector to look surprised, but he didn't. He knew more about Shane's life than she did, and that hurt. She saw him out and then came back to the tree. As everyone unwrapped their gifts, she pulled Angel aside.

"So, you have decided to leave New York, Angel?" Kathleen asked.

"Yes. Shane has the money for the tickets, and he said Bridget might be able to help me find a job. I am good with children,

I can cook—Jewish food, but I can learn, and I can keep a house."

Kathleen wasn't sure what plans had been made for the train yet. She would have to speak to Bridget. Hopefully, there was something they could work out for this girl who had risked so much.

"I am sure we will be able to find something for you to do," Kathleen told her. "For now, try to relax and enjoy yourself. I know you don't celebrate Christmas like we do, but it's fun to watch the children get so excited. You did a great job of wrapping the presents."

"Thank you," Angel said, blushing. "Not just for saying that, but for being so kind to me. Shane said you would be, but I wasn't convinced. There hasn't been a lot of good history between my people and yours."

"I like people as individuals, Angel, not because of where they come from or what religion they follow. Our mam brought us up to believe everyone was equal. The Bible doesn't say 'love thy neighbor, only if he is a certain color or nationality'."

Kathleen was distracted when she saw Kenny walk up to collect his present. She moved forward to watch his face when he saw what he had been given. Bridget had insisted he get two little red fire engines, but she wouldn't explain why, and she was curious.

Kenny beamed when he opened his present which held two small red fire engines. He gave one to Kathleen to hold before asking for quiet. Everyone fell silent.

"This is for you, George. I broke yours by accident and asked Santa to bring me one, so I could replace it."

"You did?" George said, his eyes shining.

"Yes," Kenny admitted. "I am really sorry for breaking your other one."

George burst into tears, and it took a while to convince Kenny he was crying tears of joy.

Next up was Sammy the street boy. Tommy and Mike were staying with

Granny for Christmas but had dropped off Sammy's present the night before. The look on the child's face when he opened the box to reveal a pair of slightly worn shoes was priceless. He insisted on putting them on immediately, although his gift had included socks and other underclothes for him as well. Kathleen brushed away a tear at the boy's expression, as he showed off his new shoes.

Everyone got new gifts, including Angel, who was presented with one of Lily's better-made scarves and a new, red shawl made of the finest wool from Shane. Kathleen received a couple of books, together with some personal items, including a box of perfumed soaps from Richard. She was more than a little disappointed the box hadn't contained a ring, but she put on a brave face so no one would know.

He seemed to like the books she had bought him, although he didn't spend as much time looking at the *Guide to Surgery* as she thought he might.

CHAPTER 67

*D*inner passed quickly as the entire group sat down to eat together. Cook was given pride of place at the head of the table, much to her embarrassment. She wore her new apron with pride and insisted on wearing her new slippers, saying nobody could see them.

Once everyone ate their fill, Bridget and Kathleen made up some baskets from the leftover food. Tommy and Mike would call later to collect them and pass them out to families in need. Kathleen had included some gifts of gloves, scarves, and underwear. For Granny, they had a basket made up specially, and in addition to food and clothing, they had included a box of chocolate fudge made by Cook. Kathleen had debated taking Kenny with her to give Granny the gift in person but had decided not to, as it may upset him to visit his old home.

Tommy and Mike arrived just as they sat down to play some games with the children. The men came in and admired the tree, playing with the children for a little bit before excusing themselves and saying they had to get back. Kathleen and Bridget brought them out to the kitchen to collect the food baskets. Tommy asked Shane to come into the kitchen too. Shane's face was a picture. You would think he had been asked to leave Angel's side for a year, rather than a few minutes, but Tommy was insistent he needed to speak to him.

Kathleen's stomach churned, wondering what news Tommy had brought with him.

There was something behind his request to speak to them.

"You can stop worrying. It's good news." Mike grinned at Kathleen before grabbing a mince pie from the kitchen table. "Your cook certainly knows the way to a man's heart."

"She does, but tell us what's the news?" Kathleen didn't want to be rude, but she had to know.

"Monk Eastman isn't a threat anymore. At least not once you get Angel away."

"He isn't going to come after her? But what of Lucky's debts? He must want revenge." Shane echoed her own thoughts, but she didn't want to alarm her brother, so she stayed silent, waiting to hear what Tommy knew.

"We may have spread a rumor Angel has already left. She went to her aunt's place as Haviv insisted she should, Haviv being the oldest now that Axel is dead."

Her hand flew to her mouth. Richard hadn't told her his patient had died.

"Easy, Kathleen. Axel will be fine. He is going to disappear too. But it was easier if Monk believed him to be dead."

"So they are all safe?" Kathleen wished her heart would slow down a bit. "Oh, Tommy, Mike, we owe you so much already, and you go and do this for us too."

Tommy turned the color of Santa's suit, while Mike pushed another mince pie into his mouth.

"We didn't do nothing special."

Despite Tommy's protests, Kathleen knew the boys had taken a big risk. If Monk found out they were lying, he would make them pay.

"I am so glad you men came into our lives. We are so much richer for it. Will you come for dinner on New Year's day? Cook is rustling up another feast as Father Nelson and Inspector Griffin couldn't be here today."

Mike's eyes nearly took over his face. "We'll be here. That woman can cook."

Everyone laughed, before Kathleen and Bridget hugged Tommy and Mike close.

"Thank you for looking after my family," Bridget whispered. Tommy's red face didn't go any paler, as Bridget kissed his cheek. The poor man nearly ran out the back door, Mike following after him with the baskets piled up one on top of the other.

"Shane, Angel will be safe in Riverside Springs. Are you going to travel with us?"

"Yes, Bridget. I best go tell Angel the news, since she was very worried about Monk. She thought she was putting the sanctuary and all of you in danger by being here."

Shane left Kathleen and Bridget in the kitchen.

"Sit a while. You look like you had a shock, and you don't want to alarm the children."

Kathleen knew Bridget was right. She was shocked but pleased. Nobody wanted Monk Eastman's attention, and she was thrilled Angel would get to live out her life in the peace of Riverside Springs. Shane, too.

"Mrs. Grayson will give Angel a home, and Bella may be able to give her a job. Something will work out. Shane can work with Geoff Rees once his arm heals, until he saves up enough money to set up his own place." Bridget looked closely at Kathleen. "What are your plans?"

She didn't get a chance to respond, as George came running in.

"You are missing all the fun, Miss Kathleen. Miss Lily said you were to come back, the both of you."

They spent the afternoon relaxing and playing games with the children. In the evening, the group gathered around the Christmas tree as Richard lifted Kenny up to put the star at the top. George had won the right to put the ornament on the tree but had nominated Kenny to do it in his place. He said Kenny needed some good luck and should make a wish.

Kenny smiled for the first time since the

funeral. Richard held her hand as the little boy wished for a new home with a mother and father who liked dogs. Kathleen took a deep breath. She wished she could offer this amazing little boy a home, but she wasn't at that stage in her life yet.

"I wish the same thing," Richard whispered in her ear. "But I think Kenny would benefit from leaving New York. There are too many bad memories here. He will thrive elsewhere."

She nodded to acknowledge his comment, but she wasn't at all sure the boy would thrive. If he was lucky and got parents who accepted Jack and him, he might. But it was hard enough finding decent people to adopt little children, without asking them to adopt a dog as well.

She glanced over at Shane and Angel. They were also holding hands, and the look of love on their faces was obvious for everyone to see. They were too young to get married, but she was certain, as soon as Angel came of age, they would.

"Are you happy with the way the day turned out?" Bridget asked, coming to stand beside her.

"Yes. It was wonderful, wasn't it? The children were so excited. Everything worked out perfectly."

"It did," Bridget said, staring at Kenny with a soft smile on her face.

"He is a wonderful little boy, isn't he? I hope you can find him a nice family when you leave on the next train."

"Actually, Kathleen, Carl and I want to speak to Lily and you about that. Could you tear yourself away, so we can speak in the office?"

Surprised, Kathleen agreed. She looked around for Richard to tell him where she was going, but he seemed to have disappeared. Maybe he was in the office already.

CHAPTER 68

*H*e wasn't, but Carl, Charlie, and Lily were. Kathleen sat down beside Lily, as Bridget joined her husband standing opposite the sofa.

"Kathleen, Carl and I have decided this next orphan train will be our last trip."

"What? But I thought you were feeling better. Did Richard say something was wrong?"

"No, he didn't. He just repeated what he had already told us. I need to rest more and look after my heart. It won't take the strain of all the traveling. While I love my job, it does take a lot out of me, especially saying goodbye to all the lovely children we meet. So," Bridget glanced at Carl who took her hand in his, "we've decided to settle in Riverside Springs. We would be near to Liam and Annie. Shane, too, assuming Angel's and his plans work out."

Kathleen stood up and gave her sister a hug.

"I will miss you, and the children will too. You won't be easy to replace," Kathleen said before adding, "but I want you to be happy and healthy."

"Thank you."

"I almost wish I could go live in Riverside Springs. All my favorite people seem to end up living there," Lily said, tears making her eyes bright.

"Kathleen, we have another suggestion for you," Bridget said. "We would like to give Kenny and Jack a home. We know adoption is out of the question until they find Kenny's mother, but we don't care. We have fallen in love with him."

Kathleen didn't know what to say. It was like everything she had prayed for was coming true.

"We think it's wonderful, don't we, Kathleen?" Lily prompted as the silence lingered.

"Sorry, yes, of course it is. Kenny will be over the moon, but are you sure you know what you are taking on in Jack? That dog is mad."

Carl and Bridget laughed with everyone else.

"We know, but we hope he can be trained," Bridget said.

Kathleen didn't hold out much hope for that, but given how much her sister already adored the dog, she didn't think it would matter.

"When are you going to tell Kenny?" Kathleen asked.

"We thought we would leave it until to-morrow. He's had enough excitement for one day," Bridget said.

"Oh, I think he wouldn't mind a little

more. Did you hear what he wished for when he put the star on the tree? I think you should go tell him now."

"You do?" Bridget's expression showed her how much her sister was dying to tell the child. "Is that all right with you, Lily?"

"It's perfect. What a lovely way to end Christmas day," Lily said.

A knock interrupted them, and Richard popped his head in.

"Sorry to interrupt, folks, but could I drag Kathleen away for a few minutes?" Richard asked.

Everyone looked at her as her cheeks flamed with embarrassment.

"Yes," she answered, as she let him walk her out of the office and toward the back of the sanctuary. She looked out the window to the garden, seeing a tree decorated with candles. She looked at Richard, whose eyes were sparkling with mischief.

"I thought you might enjoy a private, Christmas tree, do you like it?"

"I love it. It's magical."

CHAPTER 69

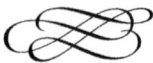

"Here, put this on, so you don't get cold." He wrapped her warm shawl around her shoulders, and to-gether, they walked outside to the tree, its pine scent wafting up her nose. She gazed up in wonder, as she counted the candles. It looked fabulous and seemed even more magical when standing beside it.

"Kathleen," he spoke so softly she almost didn't hear him. She turned to find him with one knee on the ground.

"Richard, you'll get wet."

"I messed up the first time I asked you.

This time I want to do it right," he said softly. "Kathleen Collins, will you do me the honor of becoming my wife?" He held out a small, velvet-covered box, opening it to show her a dazzling diamond ring. It looked like the candles on the tree. She tried to take it in her hands, but they were shaking too badly.

"Yes," she said, as he stood up. He took her finger and placed the ring on it, and then he reached down and kissed her sweetly.

"I love you, Miss Collins. I promise never to try to tell you what to do again."

"I love you too, Richard. I promise to try not to be too stubborn, although I have to say, it's a family trait."

He took her in his arms and kissed her again and again.

"I suppose I should return you to your meeting," he said. "It was rude of me to tear you away."

"Oh, no, it had almost finished. Bridget and Carl want to adopt Kenny, well they want to foster him until the time comes when they can make it official. Bridget told me she is finally taking your advice—they are going to live in Riverside Springs. This next trip will be their last."

"I hope you don't blame me for that decision. I know it won't be easy with your sister living so far away."

"Blame you?" Kathleen said, surprised. "How could I when it was your expertise that saved her life. I love you, Richard."

She held her head up for another kiss and another. Each kiss melted away the doubts she had about where she should live. Her place was by his side, no matter where he chose to be.

"I will live wherever you want. If you want to be with your family in Riverside Springs, I can set up a practice out there. I don't care where I am, so long as you are at my side."

"Oh, Richard, I was just thinking the same. I will live wherever you want."

He smiled as he circled her with his

arms, drawing her close against him. They stood looking at the candles for a few minutes. Then he looked down at her.

"I believe the children of New York need our help, but I might be biased, given the hospitals are here."

"I think the same," Kathleen agreed. "I would love to see Bridget and my other siblings more often, but the children do need us. Not just the orphans, but those on the street. We can help them, just like Lily, Mrs. Fleming, Father Nelson, and Inspector Griffin helped my family."

"Then we will stay here, but perhaps we can have a house of our own. I love your orphans, but I rather like the idea of spending some time alone with my wife," Richard said.

"I like the sound of that, too."

They kissed some more until the sweet sound of Silent Night filled the air.

"The children were practicing with Sheila. They sound wonderful, don't they?" she said, torn between wanting to stay with him at their magical tree and going back inside to see the children sing.

"We should go back inside before you freeze to death. Some doctor I am, letting my future wife get hypothermia."

Giggling, she waited, as he put out the candles.

"I can't let the tree start a fire. I want Lily to like me."

"She likes you a lot already," Kathleen assured him. "She will like you even more now we have decided to live in New York. She was afraid I would go to Riverside Springs too. Her heart is tied to Carmel's Mission."

"She's done an incredible job here—really the sanctuary should be called Lily's Mission. Why did she call it Carmel's?"

"It's named after Charlie's grandmother, who is a formidable woman. She lived around here until the blizzard back in '88, after which she moved to Colorado. She inspired Lily a lot."

"She sounds like a woman I would like

to meet. Maybe she will come to visit sometime."

"Charlie has invited her to come see her great-grandchildren, so you may get your wish soon."

"We better get inside, or the kids will have finished their song. Just one more thing," he said.

"What?"

"This," he smiled, before kissing her deeply again. "I don't think I will ever have enough of kissing you."

CHAPTER 70

Kenny looked up at the star on top of the tree. The day was nearly over, and all his wishes hadn't come true. Santa hadn't given him back Mary and his ma, but at least he had made Kathleen come and save him from Lucky. And he had Jack. That was good. He glanced at George who was almost asleep on the floor, his small, red, fire engine held tightly in his hand.

The door opened, and Kathleen and the doctor came in, their faces all red. They looked happy, though. Everyone was. It was Christmas, after all.

"Kathleen, I thought you would never come back in. We were waiting for you," Bridget chided her sister. Kenny checked Bridget's face, but she was still smiling. She didn't get mad like his ma.

"Sorry, Bridget, that was my fault," the doctor said. "I finally did things properly and am glad to announce we are properly engaged."

Soon everyone was crying again and hugging Kathleen and her doctor. Adults could be weird sometimes. Jack barked a few times, and his tail wagged. Kenny passed him another treat. Cook had made Jack his own special sausages, just for Christmas.

His eyes closed again, but then he felt himself being picked up. He knew that smell. It was Bridget holding him. He opened his eyes, trying to concentrate.

"Kenny, I have something to ask you. Can you wake up?"

He tried to say yes, but Jack answered first by barking. Everyone laughed but Bridget. She looked serious. His belly got a little sore, and he wondered if something was wrong. Was she going to say goodbye today? He'd heard she was going to somewhere called Springs. Mary would kill him, if she knew how often he listened at the doors. Maybe she did know. Someone said those in Heaven could see him.

"Kenny, Carl and I would like you and Jack to come live with us in Riverside Springs. Would you like that?"

"Me?"

"You and Jack. We want both of you to come."

"You mean it?" he asked, his stomach turning over. "You really do?"

"Yes, darling, we really do. We can't adopt you until we find your ma and ask her permission, but that doesn't matter. We love you and Jack and never want to lose you. So, what do you say?"

"Santa really is magic. He gave Jack and

me a home, just like I asked. I love you too," Kenny whispered, as he wound his arms around Bridget's neck.

Jack barked and jumped up on both of them, pushing his nose into their hug. Kenny knew this would be the best Christmas of his life, no matter how long he lived.

EPILOGUE

CHRISTMAS, 1896

Kathleen bit her lip, trying to stop the fluttering in her stomach.

"You look beautiful," Bridget said, as she fussed at Kathleen's veil.

"Richard won't be able to keep his eyes off you." Lily agreed, as she stood to the side, holding baby Grace in her arms. Kathleen's goddaughter was almost a year old but thankfully was an easy-going baby. Lily's almost two-year-old twins Teddy and Laurie were a handful.

"I can't believe you are all here with me

to celebrate. I couldn't believe it when you came in the door, Bridget, with Kenny, Liam, and Annie at your side."

"Annie wasn't going to miss the opportunity of being a bridesmaid. Carolyn said she even helped stitch her dress."

Bella came forward with a spray of ivy and some winter flowers for her bouquet.

"Charlie Doherty and Carl planned this with Richard, as his wedding present to you. You are marrying a wonderful man, Kathleen. I am so happy for you."

Kathleen smiled at Bella, glowing in the late stages of pregnancy. Her baby was due in March, and Brian kept telling everyone it would be a boy. Bella had confided her husband was quite envious of Lily's twins and hoped they would be blessed with a set of twins too. Kathleen knew her friend would prefer to have one baby to start with.

"This is for you." Angel came forward with a beautiful silver bracelet. "I want to lend it to you for your special day. It is supposed to bring you luck." Angel caught the laughs of the other women. "I mean, not that you need good luck, but…"

"It's lovely, thank you," Kathleen leaned in to give Angel a kiss on her cheek. The Jewish girl had blossomed in her time in Riverside Springs and was training to take over for the schoolteacher who had decided to retire. Shane was so proud of his young wife-to-be.

"Thank you, all, for everything, for being my sister and my friends. I love you so much."

"Don't start crying. You will ruin your face," Bridget chided, but her own eyes were sparkling with unshed tears.

"Can I come in?" a male voice asked from the doorway.

"Yes, Charlie, just in time to stop the river of tears," Lily replied to her husband.

Charlie Doherty stared at Kathleen, a large smile lighting up his face.

"You look stunning, Kathleen Collins. I am honored to give you away today."

Kathleen smiled back, thankful this kind

man who had done so much to help her family had agreed to walk her down the aisle. Father Nelson had helped prepare Richard for the wedding.

The women went ahead of them to the church, leaving her alone with Charlie for a few minutes.

"I hope you will be as happy as Lily and I are," he said offering her his arm. She nodded, too choked up to speak. He escorted her out of the sanctuary into the waiting cab. Thankfully, it was a beautiful winter's day with the sun shining in a clear, blue sky. She glanced back at the home she had enjoyed for so long. She would live in Richard's brownstone but would come back to the sanctuary often. Richard was happy for her to continue her work with the women and children of New York.

As they arrived at the church, they could hear the strains of the music playing. Charlie helped her out of the cab and walked her into the church. One last surprise awaited her. A group of children all dressed in their Sunday best stood waiting to walk up the aisle in front of her.

"Oh, my word, you are all here. I can't believe it," Tears came to her eyes as she greeted Megan and Eileen, the twins bearing little resemblance to the young girls she had met at the Flemings. Sally and Lizzie were standing with her younger sister, Annie. Her brother Liam stood close to Kenny.

Kenny tugged at her arm and whispered, "They made Jack sit outside, but he's happy. Granny Belbin gave him a big bone."

"How does Jack like life in the country?" she asked Kenny.

"He loves it. He's got a wife and a family of his own now. Mam says he can't have any more children, though, as she doesn't know where to put them all."

Kathleen could hear Bridget saying that, but she knew her sister would give Kenny almost anything he wanted.

Charlie took her arm and walked her slowly to the front of the packed church.

She could barely see for the tears of happiness flowing down her face. Everyone who meant anything to her seemed to be here. Dave Fleming, his son Colm, and the girls. Jacob, Lizzie's older brother, sat with his adoptive parents. Carolyn and Geoff Rees beamed at her, as did Inspector Griffin and his wife. Cook, Jane, and the other members of the sanctuary team were sitting with Granny Belbin, who amazingly enough wasn't wearing black. Tommy and Mini Mike were also wearing suits and looked so uncomfortable she almost felt sorry for them. Shane sat beside Angel in the front row beside Bridget, Lily, and the rest of her family.

She walked to the altar, where Richard stood with Carl as his best man and Patrick, the orphan they planned on officially adopting once they got married. Despite his new clothes, Patrick looked exactly the same as the cheeky child who'd stolen her heart on the trip to find her brothers.

Father Nelson smiled and made jokes

during the service as he married them. The words passed over her, and she couldn't have repeated any of them as Richard held her gaze. His hand was warm taking hers yet sending shivers through her body. He was her husband.

The choir sang "Silent Night" as they walked down the aisle, husband and wife at last.

"Are you happy, Mrs. Green?" he whispered.

She nodded, wishing he would kiss her. He seemed to read her mind, as his lips closed over hers in the lightest of kisses. Then holding hands, they left the church to head back to the sanctuary for the party.

"You look so happy, Kathleen. I am thrilled things worked out so well for you," Lily said as the women sat in the living room, the men having stayed in the dining room to enjoy the cigars Richard had provided. The children were all, thankfully, in bed asleep, even Grace and the twins.

"We have all come so far since that day

we ran from Oaks, a day we thought was the worst of our lives yet turned out to be a blessing," Bridget said, a smile playing around her lips. Kathleen looked at her sister more closely. She had the feeling Bridget was hiding something.

"This place changed all of our lives for the better, and it's all thanks to you, Lily Doherty," Bella commented, shifting slightly in her seat.

"Carmel's Mission is a success because of women like you. All of you. I am so proud to call you my friends, Bridget, Bella, and you, too, Angel. We miss you, but we know you are happy with our new friends in Riverside Springs. Kathleen, I know it's selfish of me, but I am so glad Richard is staying on at his practice in New York. I would miss you too much if you went to live in Wyoming too."

"Richard is a city boy, and I guess I am a city girl," Kathleen said, wondering if this bubble of happiness was ever going to burst. She had everything she wanted. She was the luckiest girl in the world.

"I think Carl, Kenny, and myself may try living in the city for a little while," Bridget said, her face glowing.

"Why?" Lily asked. Kathleen and Bella said, "What?"

"We think my new brother-in-law would be the best person to help Kenny's brother or sister come into this world." Bridget's hands rested gently on her stomach.

"Bridget Collins, are you telling us you are having a baby?" Lily demanded, standing up to give Bridget a hug.

"It's Bridget Watson, and, yes, I believe I am."

Kathleen hugged her sister close.

"I hope you don't think I ruined your day. I wanted to tell you, but it wasn't fair to steal your thunder on your wedding day. Only I am so excited I think I could burst," Bridget spoke quickly.

"Of course, I don't think that. I am

thrilled. We all are. So, will you stay in New York or go back to Riverside Springs after the baby is born?"

"We will go back. Riverside Springs is our home, and Kenny has made so many new friends. But Carl insists Richard is the one to deliver the baby. He says I owe my life to Richard, and he is the only one he trusts to look after me. Richard is a very special man."

"I do hope you are not trying to dispel any fears my wife may have, as it's a bit too late for her to change her mind," Richard joked, as the men joined them. Carl came to his wife's side and sat beside her. Charlie took a seat beside Lily, while Brian, Bella, Shane, and Angel shared the sofa.

"Looks like there is no room for us, darling. Shall we go home?"

Blushing furiously, as her friends and family teased her, Kathleen looked into his eyes.

"Yes, please," she said, rising on tippy toes to kiss him. "Thank you for making today the best day of my life," she whispered into his ear.

"My pleasure. I love you, Kathleen Green," he whispered back, before picking her up and carrying her out to the cab waiting to take them home.

ACKNOWLEDGMENTS

This book wouldn't have been possible without the help of so many people. Thanks to Erin for my fantastic covers. Erin is a gifted artist who makes my characters come to life.

I have an amazing editor and several proofreaders. But sometimes errors slip through. I am very grateful to the ladies from my readers group who give me feedback on every book. They support my work by sharing online. Please join my Facebook group for readers of Historical fiction. Come join us for chats, prizes, exclusive content, and first looks at my latest releases. Rachel's readers group

Last, but by no means least, huge thanks

and love to my husband and our three children. And Gracie, our dog.

Orphan Train Tragedy

Orphan Train Strike

Orphan Train Disaster

Trail of Hearts - Oregon Trail Series

Oregon Bound (book 1)

Oregon Dreams (book 2)

Oregon Destiny (book 3)

Oregon Discovery (book 4)

Oregon Disaster (book 5)

12 Days of Christmas - co -authored series.

The Maid - book 8

Clover Springs Mail Order Brides

Katie (Book 1)

Mary (Book 2)

Sorcha (Book 3)

Emer (Book 4)

Laura (Book 5)

Ellen (Book 6)

Thanksgiving in Clover Springs (book 7)

Christmas in Clover Springs (book8)

Erin (Book 9)

Eleanor (book 10)

Cathy (book 11)

Mrs. Grey

Clover Springs East

New York Bound (book 1)

New York Storm (book 2)

New York Hope (book 3)

Printed in Great Britain
by Amazon